WHAT the NIGHT SINGS

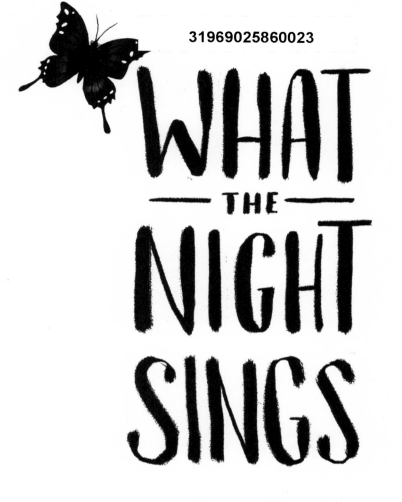

WHAT THE NIGHT SINGS

A NOVEL

VESPER STAMPER

Alfred A. Knopf · New York

All rights reserved. Published in the United States by Alfred A. Knopf,
an imprint of Random House Children's Books, a division of
Penguin Random House LLC, New York.

Knopf, Borzoi Books, and the colophon are registered trademarks of
Penguin Random House LLC.

"My Dreams Are Getting Better All the Time" by Vic Mizzy and Manny Curtis,
reprinted with permission from Next Decade Entertainment, Inc.

Visit us on the Web! GetUnderlined.com

Educators and librarians, for a variety of teaching tools, visit us at
RHTeachersLibrarians.com

Library of Congress Cataloging-in-Publication Data
Names: Stamper, Vesper, author.
Title: What the night sings / Vesper Stamper.
Description: First edition. | New York : Alfred A. Knopf, [2018] | Summary:
Liberated from Bergen-Belsen concentration camp in 1945, sixteen-year-old
Gerta tries to make a new life for herself, aided by Lev, a fellow
survivor, and Michah, who helps Jews reach Palestine.
Identifiers: LCCN 2017020646 (print) | LCCN 2017037126 (ebook) |
ISBN 978-1-5247-0038-6 (trade) | ISBN 978-1-5247-0039-3 (lib. bdg.) |
ISBN 978-1-5247-0040-9 (ebook)
Subjects: | CYAC: Refugees—Fiction. | Holocaust, Jewish
(1939-1945)—Fiction. | Jews—Fiction. | Survival—Fiction. |
Germany—History—1945–1955—Fiction.
Classification: LCC PZ7.1.S732 (ebook) | LCC PZ7.1.S732 Wh 2018 (print) | DDC
[Fic]—dc23

The text of this book is set in 10.7-point Palatino.
The illustrations in this book were rendered in ink wash,
white gouache, and graphite, toned digitally.

MANUFACTURED IN CHINA
February 2018
10 9 8 7 6 5 4 3 2 1

First Edition

Random House Children's Books supports the First Amendment
and celebrates the right to read.

זכר

Remember

1

LIBERATION

Bergen-Belsen Concentration Camp

April 15, 1945

CHAPTER 1

I am lying next to Rivkah in the bunk when the announcement comes. She is burning; she is freezing. I hold her, and I sing to her:

Az ir vet, kinderlekh, elter vern, vet ir aleyn farshteyn—
When, dear children, you grow older, you will understand
   for yourselves—

I learned this Yiddish song from another musician on my transport here. I only spoke German before, though I sang in many other languages. When they came for me, I was rehearsing Bach's *St. Matthew Passion,* but even in German I understood nothing except the language of music. But now what do I care? I may as well die singing. Typhus is sweeping everyone away anyway. Die this way, die that way; pass out at hard labor, or get shot shuffling from one mysterious mound to the next—what's the difference?

So I hold Rivkah, and I mutter the song.

I am nearly sixteen years old. At least I think so.

Rivkah is my fourth bunkmate in Bergen-Belsen. Somehow I've survived four these last few wretched months. The first was a sick old woman from one of the death marches. She had diabetes and died from a seizure. We were packed so tightly that she shook against me for twenty minutes. I felt my brain shake in my skull; I felt my stomach shake behind my ribs. We pushed her body to the floor and folded her arms. Someone muttered a prayer over her and we fell back to sleep. It was the most dignity we could give her.

There was no time to learn her name.

The next two girls were pretty, even younger than me. This was obviously their first camp—hard to believe after so much war. It was a crowded week of transports, and the three of us shared one blanket. They kept to themselves and had managed to smuggle in a tube of lipstick. The girls were always whispering and putting on the lipstick, pinching their cheeks and ringing my ears with their acidic giggling. I didn't understand their language, but I

understood the tone: a stupid survival plot, as if they actually had a say in their fate. They starved a little more slowly than the rest of us, but one day they disappeared, one in the morning, the other that night.

Rivkah came two days later from the Buna factory. She is also from Köln, the city where I was born, and she knew my parents. She's a laboratory scientist, the mother of two boys, Michah and Chaim, fond of boxing. She said she usually scolded them for fighting, but she was secretly proud of her strong sons. They'd buy her little trinkets with the winnings from their after-school fights—flowers, chocolates—and kiss and flatter her to keep her from fussing too much. Big, sweet boys. She lost them to a transport last year but believes with her whole heart that they will all be reunited. Meanwhile, I'm a temporary substitute, a foster child. Somehow she is always smiling, even in fever. I think she's in shock—or maybe she's the kind of person who smiles so much, her face is fixed with a permanent grin, in her eyes as much as on her lips.

Rivkah had met my parents a few times at the club in Köln. My mother died in the raid on the club, I told her. She was sorry, she said. Her voice got raspy and she used her little, growing cough as an excuse not to finish her thought. A couple of weeks after Rivkah came here to Bergen-Belsen, the typhus took root. Now she is dying in my arms.

The soldiers burst into the barracks, and I keep singing. I'm dazed. I am catching fever and I don't recognize their uniforms.

Soldiers are soldiers. Guns are guns. Language is language.

They shout to us in English, with British accents, I think, muffled through the rags they hold over their noses and mouths. I'm so used to the smell of filth and death that only when I see those handkerchiefs am I reawakened to the true state of things. I'm inexplicably ashamed. I have nothing left to be ashamed about—but I pull my uniform shirt lower over my bare thighs anyway.

The soldiers begin removing the dead. There are so many. How could I not have noticed them lying right next to me?

And suddenly—Rivkah, too, is gone.

I feel her final breath wisp across my lips. They pull her from me, but I can't let her go. She is my last connection to the living world. I clutch her arm, her hand, her fingers. I sing the lullaby after her, my foster mother. I know no one else in all of Bergen-Belsen, either from Auschwitz or Theresienstadt. Everyone has come and gone, piles of shells pulled in and out of waves, and I'm still here, a skeleton of a sea creature, dropped in this tide pool, living, watching, still living.

CHAPTER 2

Two soldiers extract me from the bunk like a splinter. I'm still mumbling the song as one of them wraps me in a dirty blanket and the other picks me up like a sick baby. He carries me out of the barracks into the blinding sunshine. Every thirty seconds, I fade into blackness and reemerge. I don't feel the soldier's arms under me or the roughness of his uniform lapel on my cheek. Through a tunnel of washy sounds, I hover just above his arms, floating on a current above this chaos.

Strange I hadn't noticed it before, the bodies strewn in the courtyard. An old man who sat down to die against a wall. A woman stroking the hair of the lifeless friend in her lap. The nearly dead call out for help, reaching up to soldiers rushing by, and die with their hands in the air. People are running in zigzags. Several fall under the feet of frenzied crowds. Children wander blindly through piles of limbs and breasts that might have been mothers, open eyes, gaping mouths—I'm looking into a mirror at myself, my eyes half-lidded, my spirit exiting, entering through my mouth, making no commitment.

I'm suddenly afraid that I'm being put into another selection, and I wonder, *Who have I offended now, just by being?* Until I was captured, I had no idea I was even Jewish. I held the *Ahnenpass,* the certificate of racial purity. It stated I was Gerta Richter, four grandparents deep in Aryan blood.

The soldier lays me down on the ground inside a green tent, looks at me—looks away. His forehead is wrinkled. The rag tied around his nose and mouth is damp from sweat and tears. I see why: I am contagion. I am a threat to his life even as he saves mine. And he will handle hundreds of us today, carry us to the tent, touch our skin and clothes, breathe our miasma.

Under the olive-green sunlight I lie here. I feel the dirt; I caress the dirt; I pack the dirt under my nails, as deep as it will go. I sing—". . . *vet ir aleyn farshteyn*—" but a flutter, barely perceptible, arises in my throat, and suddenly, silence. My dry lips hang open; my voice has finally given out.

There is a boy—a man?—lying on the ground next to me. I've been in women's barracks for so long, I've forgotten what it feels like to be near one. He is another skeleton, but even in their dark hollows, his eyes are bright, hazel like my father's. He looks like a marionette, with glass eyes and a smile painted over his skin-wrapped skull. He apparently isn't sick, just starved. He has the beginnings of a shock of red hair. He speaks.

"We are free."

I turn to look at him, this madman. I must be delirious; he is speaking nonsense.

"I can see you don't believe me. But it's true. The British. They're rounding up the SS. We are free." This stranger inches his hand over to mine and grasps it.

I am staring at him, and his face morphs into abstract shapes, and I think, *This is reality; everything is made of shapes; no one is human; language is shapes.* I fade in and out again and find I've scratched the dirt with my free hand until my papery fingertips are raw and bleeding. This is the moment I understand.

I have survived.

The boy next to me stays only three days. With a little food in him, he is strong enough to get up and help the soldiers. He seems to have taken an interest in me and comes back to visit, to spoon soup into my mouth and wipe it from my chin. There is something familiar in his eyes, but I can't name it. It might be . . . kindness.

"Guten Morgen!" he greets me. "How about some soup?"

I can't speak, but he tells me in his rough, rushed German what is going on outside in the stabbing sunshine. "You've never seen a thing like it," he says, lifting the spoon to my lips. "When they opened the camp, it's like the SS knew they were coming. They just exchanged commanders: yesterday, SS—today, British. The guards even tried to blend in with us, in camp uniforms. But they couldn't get away with that. And everyone is dying, dying . . . and there are too many to bury. So today they rounded up the guards and made them dig huge new pits. And in one of those pits, do you know what they did?" Here he catches a potato and maneuvers it into my mouth. "The soldiers made the guards lie with their faces in the dirt, like corpses. They had to lie there with guns at the back of their necks for the longest time. And when they were allowed to climb out, they had to carry each body from the piles by hand and bury it and say, 'Rest in peace'!"

I realize I'm smiling at the thought. My jaw feels a little looser as I chew. The boy pats my shoulder, strokes my forehead and pulls the blanket back over me.

CHAPTER 3

I've been in this tent ten days, and I make no decision to walk out; my brain just lifts me, and I leave. A British nurse grabs my arm and I feel the sickening lack of muscle, the bare nerve rolling between my skin and bone.

"Your name?" she asks. I have to think a moment.

My *name*?

"I'm glad you're able to get up," she says, "and you're free to leave the medical tent, but I need your name so I can write that you've gone."

I pull up the sleeve on my left arm and show her the tattoo of my number: *A28865.* She begins writing it on a card.

"All right, that's helpful, too, but, my dear, I really do need to know your name. Oh, and your place of residence before the war."

I blink halfway, swallow, moisten my lips. "Rausch," I say, the first word since I lost my voice on the day of liberation. "Gerta . . . Rausch. Würzburg." I walk away into the afternoon sun.

"Wait, Gerta Rausch!" She is frantic, calling after me. "They are moving everyone out of the barracks! You'll need to get a new bed assignment!"

But I'm almost across the courtyard now. There are still mounds of bodies waiting to be buried, like cordwood or piles of matchsticks. Men with religion emerge to say Kaddish, the mourner's prayer, as the dirt is packed over and patted down. I never learned any prayers, so I wander away into the fields, beyond the gates and watchtowers, as far from the barracks and bodies as my atrophied muscles will carry me. My legs begin to feel their strength, and I break into what I think is a run but must be more like the shuffle of an elderly woman.

I am midway across a vast meadow, tall grass cutting my legs, before I realize I have nowhere to go.

Barbed wire edges this barren, infinite wilderness, just a line of stitching along a gray tea towel. How did such flimsy boundaries hold us here?

And if I am free, how do I get home?

And where is home?

I walk back through the gates, exhausted.

Nurses, new soldiers, relief workers ask questions among themselves in English, thinking we can't understand—

"Why did they not rise up?"

"Didn't they know?"

"Couldn't someone have armed them?"

—as though these hypotheses could be tested. As though we could have fathomed the intricacies of the Nazi web: the reinvention of language, the animalization of human souls.

As I round the corner back to the main camp road, I pass a group walking by in street clothes. For almost two years, I've seen nothing but uniforms of either captives or captors. But here now are pretty flowered spring dresses, tweed coats and trousers, crocheted sweaters on fat babies. It's so alien to my eyes, I think I must have walked into the wrong place, into some kind of Easter parade.

The British have brought our neighbors here for a visit.

Families from Winsen, Buchholz, Osterheide. I think about the transports from camp to camp, how I screamed inside as we passed village after village: *Do you know there are human beings on this train? Do you care?* But long before, it had been codified into law, digested in the guts of children along with their biscuits and milk: we weren't humans, but infectious vermin. We were simply animals in these . . . appropriate vehicles.

So now the soldiers round up the old village ladies, young mothers with their hair curled and pinned, wounded and decommissioned German soldiers. They bring them on a little excursion through the corpse-woods, past the stinking mass graves, into the storage rooms where luggage molders unclaimed and shorn hair piles up in a corner, destined to be stuffed into mattresses and woven into cloth for SS uniforms. Such things are merely the by-products of their animal neighbors. Shoes, thousands upon thousands, fill another warehouse: white kid-leather baby booties, red high-heeled dancing shoes. A closet holds the half-skeletal remains of discarded women.

Some of the visitors vomit on themselves. Hardened veterans faint. Women holding their pretty children become furious and spit their demand to leave. The soldiers won't relent. One woman is shouting so loud, a sergeant grabs her red cheeks until his fingers press them white. He yanks her head and forces her to stare into the room.

"You will look at this! You will take it in with your blind eyes until they truly see! You, you let this happen—to your own neighbors, in your own country, your own streets. These are humans! Human beings!" His mouth foams; he shakes her with all his own shock and indignation. She slaps his hand away. Her cheeks have begun to bruise.

"No," she says, her eyes wide but her voice calm. "No. They are not. They never were. This never happened."

CHAPTER 4

It's been a month since the British came. We've been moved into the SS quarters across the woods. There are still many living in the old barracks, but less crowding means at least everyone gets her own mat and blanket. We no longer have to line up outside for a supper of cloudy dishwater. Now we can

sit in shifts in the dining hall and eat a whole potato; now and then we get a little margarine.

There is a woman in the camp, a lady whose hair has grown in like patchy grass, who never stops laughing or grinning. Some fool noticed this lunatic quality and gave her the task of "boosting morale" among us. Thanks to her maddening pep, though, it may backfire. She takes her post at the door to the dining hall and greets each person with a saccharine "Good morning, good morning! How are we doing? It's a beautiful day to be alive! A little warm, a little cold, a little wet, a little dry—depends how you look at it, depends on your perspective! *Make* it a great day!"

She is like a cup of warm lemonade buzzed about with wasps. I suppose there must be a way to be friendly and kind, to laugh heartily without making people want to throw you from a bridge. I *almost* let a remark slip—

"Time and place, Gerta," my papa used to say, when my mouth would

run faster than my brain. "Wisdom is knowing the time and place." I wish I could find the time and place to pour this soup over her head.

In my daydream of Papa, I forget where I am for a moment and how weak my legs still are. The sounds around me become muffled, as though my head were under a pillow. The *ding* of metal falling on a brick floor, a *splosh* of liquid—and just before my vision goes completely dark, I feel myself caught under the arms.

I emerge back into the present to the shrieking of a woman chastising someone over the waste. My sight brightens. The shrieker is none other than the waspy-lemonade woman. It's in *my* face that she's waving her finger, as two others hold her back and remind her—

"There is plenty now—"

"We are no longer starving—"

"The soup will not bring back the dead."

Whoever has caught me turns me around: it's my friend from the medical tent. He has color in his face now, and the beginnings of red whiskers, like his hair. He's smiling softly, the many-paned window reflecting in his eyes. He sits me down at the table and hands me his own tin cup of soup.

"Go ahead; I'm not hungry," he lies. I look down into the cup. What I feel in my belly is different somehow—the hunger of someone who's suddenly remembered what fullness feels like.

"I used to be a singer," I tell him.

He looks at me, smiles, nods. "Oh," he says, unsure of how to respond. "I'm sorry, I should have asked, all this time—I don't know your name."

"Gerta. Rausch." I use my real last name, pausing a moment as I think of the lengths to which Papa went to avoid it. I attempt a handshake but he puts his hand up, politely refusing to shake it. It seems odd that this boy who held my hand in the tent, stroked my forehead and caught me when I fainted will not shake it now. "Yours?"

"Levi Goldszmit. You can call me Lev."

"Lev," I choose, with a smile. "Nice to really meet you now."

"And where are you from, Gerta Rausch?"

"I'm from Köln, but I've lived in Würzburg since I was little."

"And you were a singer, you said? *Jazz?*" He makes a vaudevillian face.

"I was studying opera."

"Opera!" he says, brightening. "Will you sing for me?"

I'm suddenly embarrassed. I haven't sung at all since the day of liberation, but *actual* singing? Not since Theresienstadt. "Not yet," I say. "I'm not ready." I point to my throat. "Takes a while to get it back."

"Well, God gave you a gift to share with the world," he says, a bit sanctimoniously, which I think he realizes. He reaches up and tugs his earlobe. "But opera? Isn't it only old ladies who sing opera?" He laughs at the thought. "How old *are* you?"

"It's May—" I calculate. "Right—I must have just turned sixteen! Imagine forgetting that. . . . You?"

"Eighteen."

I'm shocked. He looks so much older than that. I wonder if he thinks the same about me. Gone from everyone in the camp is any hint of round-faced youthfulness, from the babies, too. Our faces are chiseled stone, even with a month of food in our bellies.

"And where did you live?" I ask. "Before the war, I mean."

"I'm from Poland. My town is Kielce. But my mother is . . . was German." He looks blankly at his hands. "So I speak a little." He smiles again. "Quite well, no?"

"Getting better!" I laugh. I take a sip of the soup. Somehow it's the most delicious thing I've tasted in years.

CHAPTER 5

For two weeks, I've been treated and disinfected; I've washed and rewashed my one ratty uniform shirt. A team of American medical students comes this morning with a truck full of clothes and shoes. They dump the crates in the dining hall. Some are donations from charity drives. Some are the discards of the dead.

Two middle-aged women take the reins and organize things. They have some men arrange the tables into long rows, and everyone helps make piles of clothes: women's, men's, boys' and girls'. This brings everybody into the hall, and for the first time I see several of the other women from my orchestra at Auschwitz. We embrace, but there is nothing to say. How odd that we, of all people, would have survived.

Everyone is overtaken by an intense desire to impose order. We line shoes up by size along the benches and make signs with cardboard and sticks. Each piece of clothing is folded neatly, with reverence, especially the children's clothes, which have the most items and the fewest takers. Some take the little baby shirts just to put under their pillows, to hold like real children.

I remember my size before I was deported. I'm so much thinner, but maybe I've grown taller. I start at the end of the line and choose a brassiere and matching underpants, blue gray with a little lace along the edge. Pretty nothings from an elegant lady who had something beautiful to wear them under. Or someone to show them to.

It's been a year since I've thought about Maria Büchner, my step-mother, my maestra. She was magnificent, a goddess. I was too young to study opera, but she heard something in my voice and took a chance, shifting me toward serious study. For my debut, she gave me one of her gowns, pale green taffeta with a pleated skirt and a million crystal beads. I never did get to wear that dress. It could still be hanging on the back of the closet door at home. I clench the clothes in my hands and wonder what she did after we were taken. Did she cry for us? Did she forget us? *Could she . . . could she have been the one who turned us in?*

I shake away the thought and take a navy skirt, black dress shoes and a light blue blouse with a pattern of blossoms on it. It reminds me of the pale sky of a Würzburg summer morning, the white blossoms on the orange trees in the gardens.

I'm swimming in these clothes, still skeletal, though I know I've put on some weight in the past few weeks. I make a pleat in the front of the skirt and roll the waistband over to hold it. Under the skirt, the blouse has to be pulled down practically to my knees just to keep it fitted against me. But these are *my* clothes now, ones I chose for myself. I step out of invisibility. I have a name. I am Gerta Rausch.

I am a girl again, in clothes *I* chose, with a sky full of flowers on my blouse.

CHAPTER 6

I rummaged through a bin of clothes today, and now I have something *extra:* a silk scarf with bright yellow butterflies on it. Looking in the mirror hanging on the outside wall of the bathhouse, I wrap it stylishly around my choppy hair, with a careful knot in the middle, the ends hanging down over my right shoulder. Maria used to call it her "market look," just understated enough to make her resemble a home-maker . . . but with panache. She knew how to exude glam-our even when buying groceries, and I am ready to be pretty again, myself.

Instead, my reflection is almost comical, with my sunken cheeks and bulging eyes, framed by this yellow-and-white halo. My teeth—God—huge, protruding from my jaw. I prac-tice smiling and feel like I'm lying. I've been in the camps for almost two years, but at least ten have been added to my face.

All of us children knew only the world that our

parents opened to us. My father made the choice to hide everything from me. I was too young to question Papa's new reality or whether my childhood memories were ever real.

I'm not angry with him. Maybe I will be in time, but right until the night of our capture, I had the happiest life imaginable. We lived in music. We buttered our bread with it. Music walked in the door with Papa or Maria like another member of the family. Yes, the war was hard on everyone, but thank goodness we weren't *Jews,* I thought. How awful to be harassed, beaten and humiliated in the street, to not be allowed to work or go to school. At least that didn't apply to *us.*

It never occurred to me to ask why Papa finally stopped playing in the orchestra. Why he never left the house. Why I never went to school in Würzburg but was tutored at home. I assumed it was so I could concentrate on my training. Or because Papa was overprotective.

Maria doted on me. She was committed to helping me to understand it all: how to dress for the new curves in my figure, to put on lipstick, to make sure my armpits smelled like *Eau de Lilac* instead of *Eau de New Teen*. I just assumed the war would end and, in a seamless path, I'd go to conservatory and become a famous diva, like her.

It didn't take long after arriving in my first camp for all of that to change. Of course there was no more perfume or stylish clothing to choose from, and just as I had started my cycles, a few weeks of hunger stopped them altogether. There was nothing to manage anymore. And nothing like beauty to worry about.

Yet, on sleepless nights, we girls in Theresienstadt whispered together about the future. We still had a bit of innocence left, a sliver of hope.

"They can't keep us in here forever, right? We're just kids. As soon as we get out of here," I told them, "I'll continue my operatic training in earnest." We talked about gowns and shoes and flowers and hairstyles, and carved out of the emptiness a small mental space in which our closets and bellies were full and the road before us was straight. We couldn't have known what a luxury such thinking was.

And now I am here, decades older than fourteen. No—only two years older. My chest is as sunken as my eyes, and I wear the brassiere as nothing more than a wishful formality. I am hollow and barren and still a child, an orphan with no one to show me what to do or expect next. I have only what I can remember of Maria Büchner's advice about life:

"Find a man who will worship you, and never tell him a *thing* about yourself. And for heaven's sake, always carry red lipstick and a mirror!" How utterly ludicrous those words seem now, perched like a cheap toy on the lip of a grave. When you're dying for so long, old urgencies wither and die.

Instead, I became consumed with the business of existing.

I come back to myself. In the mirror, a dark line of cloud hangs over the barracks. They are burning.

I run back across the camp to the old courtyard, where all the inhabitants have been ushered out. The soldiers are hosing the buildings with fire. The flames just kiss the birches nearby and char the undersides of their limbs; ever after, the scars will curl under to protect the fissures left by the fire. But the trees will live and not die; they will put forth new, full leaves.

A few hundred of us watch the barracks burn until they are just pits of smoking ground.

"To stop the typhus," says a woman next to me.

"It's about time," I say, and I mean it. But there is a pang I can't name, like a part of myself is being erased.

It's over, and I start back; the faint sound over the loudspeaker announces supper. I pass the bathhouse mirror again on the way. No barracks remain in the rear view now, just a smoking road to nowhere. I stop to tidy up my novice scarf tying, yellow silk butterflies framing my bony face. Someone else appears in the mirror with me. It's Lev. He smiles, puts up his hand in a friendly wave. I return his smile and he comes closer. He is wearing a small skullcap now.

"That's a very pretty *tichel*," he says in his Polish accent. His German is really improving.

"Thank you," I say. "A what?"

"On your head—are you religious?"

"What? Oh! The scarf. No, no." I brush the suggestion away with a very Maria Büchner–style wave of the hand. "It's just—my hair, you know, it's so shaggy, it shouldn't be seen by man nor beast."

"Oh," he says. "Well, it's . . . nice."

It's strange to have a boy's eyes on me.

"I have a little affinity for butterflies." I shrug.

"Ah! So did my sister. They were always landing on her. Sometimes, if one was on her, I could get close enough to look at its eyes. They're like gems, you know, cut with facets."

"Yes, I know!" I say, the child in me suddenly taking over. "They always landed on me, too! I could even walk around with one on me and it would just stay there. There was one—a beautiful blue-and-black one—that was always at my window. I would put out my arm and it would sit on my sleeve. It would fly around my room for hours, then perch on me again. I used to think maybe it was an angel." Oh, the naïveté of those little-girl theories.

"Maybe it thought you were a flower," he says.

What a strange thing to say.

"Maybe," I answer with a jaded laugh. "A wilted, anemic flower."

"A flower waiting for rain, that's all." He stares a little. The second meal announcement comes over the loudspeaker, in German, English and Yiddish. Lev looks at me sideways.

"Walk with me to supper?"

II

WOMEN'S MUSIC

Köln

Würzburg

Theresienstadt

Auschwitz-Berkenau

Spring 1935–Fall 1944

CHAPTER 7

My papa and I walk down the cobblestone streets of Köln to the concert hall. I'm six today, walking into Papa's rehearsal with my new red dress and hair ribbon. The streets are narrow, and the second stories of the medieval houses lean over us like ancient guardians. Papa lets me carry his viola until it gets too heavy and my arms give out. I remember the first day I made the whole walk by myself, the day he didn't have to carry me in one arm and the case in the other.

I'm thinking of the piece we'll be singing in music school today, a fun Schumann chorus, and I'm suddenly transported. I see myself as a grown-up, onstage in front of hundreds. I hear the breathing, the clearing of throats, the accidental springing up of a seat as the audience adjusts and the conductor lifts his baton to begin.

I see my papa, to my left, first-chair viola. He is an old man in this vision, bow poised on string, smiling at me with wrinkles rimming his eyes. My gown moves like feathers under my fingers. I inhale.

Ich hör' meinen Schatz, den Hammer er schwinget,

Das rauschet, das klinget, das dringt in die Weite,

Wie Glockengeläute, durch Gassen und Platz.

I hear my sweetheart, the hammer he swings,

The echo, the clinking, comes to me from afar,

Like the sound of bells, through streets and squares.

"What's that tune you're humming, Gertalein?" Papa asks, stirring me
back to the street stones. I blush.

"Oh—the angel sang it to me," I say nonchalantly. I press my face to the viola case and smile to myself.

"The angel!" he says, feigning shock.

I giggle. "Yes, Papa, it's a butterfly angel."

"Does the butterfly angel visit you often?" he demands, grabbing my ribs and tickling me.

"Yes, Papa, it visits me every night!" I say through my laughter.

"Well! You must tell it something for me!" Papa pauses and kneels, looking into my eyes. Despite the hilarity a moment before, a shimmer of tears appears in his. "Tell the butterfly to always give you a song to sing. Will you demand that of your little friend?"

I touch my nose to his. "Yes, Papa."

He smiles. "And tell it to visit me with a song once in a while." He lightly pinches my earlobe, and I chuckle through the empty space where my front teeth used to be.

We arrive at the stage door. My legs feel strong, and I start humming again as I look over my shoulder at the distance we have come, without my needing to be carried, the viola case safe in my arms. Papa pushes the heavy door open and kisses the top of my head.

CHAPTER 8

It's a cool morning, and even though I'm twelve now, I don't have a choice—it's cod-liver oil and Latin recitation and the endless, tedious Wohlfahrt viola études.

But in the afternoon, it's the walk through the Residenz palace gardens, Papa and Maria on either side of me, holding my hands as we stroll to rehearsal. We always allow a bit of extra time to observe how the flowers are evolving with the seasons. I remember my first summer here in Würzburg, after that dreadful winter when I left the ghost of my mother behind in the burning city. The small town's cozy, winding streets and stooped buildings enfolded my fear like a grandmother's arms.

There was one day when we left the house and the air felt different, softer. Past the SS guards standing sentry, Papa and I walked through the scrolling iron gates, stopping at every place where a bulb pushed its new leaves through the warming ground. Everything seemed greener, more porous, as though air could flow more freely than it had only yesterday.

Around the fountain, sculptures hid like tree sprites under the topiaries—

cupids playing flutes and tambourines, or ladies dancing in their rain-worn stone gowns next to the huge pots of orange trees.

When Papa and I came to Würzburg, I joined the choir for the children of the symphony musicians. There are about forty of us now, aged six through sixteen, representing a range of ability to control our limbs and our voices. Our director is Maria Büchner herself, the renowned *Koloratursopran* diva. She also happens to be my stepmother.

She is magical. She transforms the unruly bunch of us into a heavenly host of cherubim, hovering a thousand feet above the city rooftops.

These Thursdays are outside of time, a choir in clouds. Frau Büchner wrangles impossible harmonies from our voices. Her hands flutter winglike, all of us hypnotized as she pulls notes forth from us as if spinning lace-weight yarn. New memories continue to enshroud those old ones: the fading face of my mother, a name that once was mine—what the word *Jewish* meant.

I feel a hand on my shoulder as I'm leaving the choir room.

"Gerta," says Maria, "I want to talk to you, please."

I feel my heart drop. "Yes, Maestra," I say, turning around. I use her title, not *Maria*, as I usually call her. She's always strict with me at choir rehearsal, without a trace of the affection she and I share at home. There will be no hint of favoritism here. She gestures toward a chair next to her desk. My sight-reading was terrible today, and I cannot bear to be scolded.

"Now that you are almost thirteen,

Gerta, I would like you to attempt a solo. I know you're trying to hold back, but your voice carries so clearly above your section, and I think we should capitalize on that strength—let you sing out as your voice wants to do. Am I right?"

My stomach seizes. This is what I had always wanted, of course, as I sang into the mirror every night and vocalized my school lessons, knowing I could sing better than any of the usual soloists if given the chance. But now that it comes to it, the thought of all eyes on me—

"I can see you are nervous, Gerta," the maestra says. "I know. To be chosen to stand apart from your peers is a strange feeling at first. But I will work with you. I have already spoken to your father. You will come on Tuesdays to study with me formally. I will teach you operatic technique. It is still quite early, I know. I would normally be scorned for pushing your voice too soon . . . but I don't want to wait. If we do it right, I believe you have the makings of a *dramatischer Koloratursopran*, like me." She raises her eyebrows, awaiting my assent.

"I'm honored, Maestra Büchner, of course. Thank you. But may I ask . . . when?"

"We will give it some time. You must feel ready, of course. My hope is—"

This time next year, I imagine her saying. Good. I'll have time to get used to it.

"—two months."

My eyes snap open. Why the rush? How will I overcome my dread in only *two months*? I see through her trick—this is exactly when rehearsals are to begin for the winter concert. This will be impossible.

I'm ready in three weeks.

A feeling of rightness settles into my bones, like slipping into a warm bath. I was born for this.

CHAPTER 9

I am just past fourteen when my voice changes.

We are in our last week of preparations for the spring expositions, and the maestra has given me a song from the aria book, a song of courage and passion: "Vittoria, mio core" by Carissimi. I've fallen in love with performing. I've thrown my heart all the way in. Music pours out of me, through my face and hands, all of the sorrow or ecstasy in every lyric:

> *Vittoria, vittoria, mio core!*
> *Non lagrimar più!*
> *È sciolta d'Amore la vil servitù!*
> Victory, victory, my heart!
> Don't weep anymore!
> The humiliating shackles of love are loosened!

Oh! The pangs of yearning—my heart squeezes as though I have conquered this insurmountable loss myself. For several nights now, I have dreamed of Papa's student Rudolf. Rudolf—my obsession, the object of my desire.

Well, anyway, he's a know-it-all and he walks on his toes, but he's the only boy around. He will have to do.

But Carissimi. *Carrrrrisssimi*, "dearest of darlings." Of course this aria would be written by someone with this name, the very utterance of which slays me—the trilled *rr* and knife-blade-between-the-teeth *ss* in his name. He is—I can almost see him—beckoning me from the piano. It's not old Herr Sauer accompanying rehearsal, but Carissimi himself, composing and swooning, almost fainting with desire, for *me*. He rests his head on my shoulder, a healing balm for his broken heart. *Come to me, Carrrrrisssimi. Non lagrimar più! Let me soothe your heart's wounds. Yes, yes, I will be your muse, darling! We will be poor, but we are artists, rich in love!*

But rehearsal comes to a halt—I can't reach that high F-sharp. I feel an elastic band inside my throat, stretched as tight as nature will allow, no farther. Herr Sauer plays more scales, but what I reached easily yesterday is strained and nasal today.

For the entire week, I stretch and roll my neck, I pull on my tongue from the back of my throat, I do scales up into the angelic register, but I never again sing the high F-sharp with any clarity. I forfeit the solo to Anna Müller—whom Carissimi could *never* love—and am moved into the altos. I feel the bitter defeat of Maria's dream for me. I can barely stay on pitch now; my voice is all over the place. I cry through the Easter holiday. She assures me that this is not the end of my life—mezzos can have fun, too. Because, of course, there is *Carmen*.

It is so unexpected, then, when the angel comes to my bed that night.

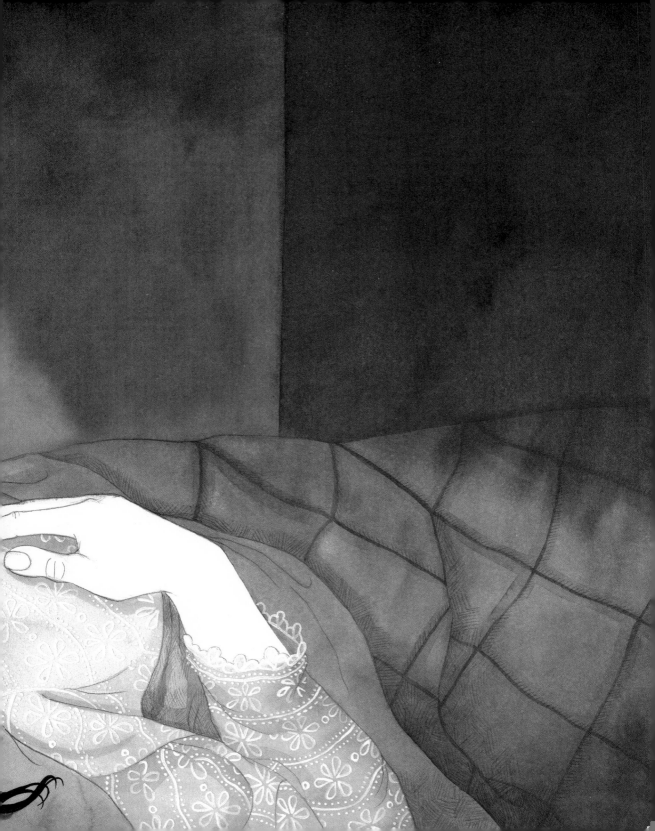

My eyes open to a blue light hovering above my Adam's apple, and the light moves down to my sternum and melts like a glacier, over and into my ribs, warm and salty. I feel a loosening of my throat, and somehow a new voice emerges, as deep and rich as chocolate. Somehow I *know* this voice, better than the soprano, which now feels like someone else's too-small dress.

My eyes close again in a deep enfolding of heavy blue blankets.

The next morning, I come into the dining room bleary-eyed. Maria is pouring tea into Papa's cup. She wishes me a good morning with the customary sleep-related questions, to which I mumble partial answers. I am hungrier than usual and devour three pieces of toast and drink two cups of tea without sitting down, wandering around the room. My stomach twinges and I am sure it's nervousness about practice that afternoon. Papa and Maria are talking in code. They have a way of hiding the true content of their conversations, thinking it's going above my head. Sometimes I try to listen in, but most of the time I'm beyond caring.

I lean over the windowsill and watch a policeman pushing an elderly woman off the sidewalk. She has a yellow star on her coat sleeve. I wonder what she must have done to deserve to be pushed like that.

Right after Maria began my training, constellations of yellow-starred people filed out of town—men, women and children carrying bundles of clothes, blankets, books tied together in stacks, weaving through the streets to the train station. I knew they were Jews, but it wasn't discussed. Not around me, anyway. I thought they were leaving by choice, just going to a safer place to wait out the war. It never bothered me that we hardly went out. I liked being home. I had Papa. I had the maestra. We had song, constant song. But on those days, we stayed inside with the lights off and the doors locked.

———————

Maria lets out a small gasp.

"Gerta, may I speak with you a moment?" she says suddenly, her eyes round, as she positions her body between Papa and me, practically herding me into the washroom. She is the maestra for a moment, not my stepmother. She closes the door behind us and speaks in a whisper.

"Gerta, look down at your nightgown. No, no, in the back."

I pull the back of my nightgown around to the front. There is blood. Come to think of it, I feel soaked. I'm frightened. What is happening? I feel faint—am I dying?

"I'm so sorry, my dear. How could I have been so thoughtless? I should have told you to expect this. Don't be afraid. This is— Well, darling, welcome to womanhood."

Maria thus begins my training in earnest, not just in opera, but in the feminine life. And just as with singing, I'm all in.

CHAPTER 10

"Let me hear the E-flat étude again, Gerta. You keep missing the A-natural in measure seven." Papa is pacing the sitting room, chewing on his pipe more than smoking it. I hear it clicking against his teeth. He's somewhere else, not really listening to my scales. I start the horrid étude again. The one drawback to being a musician's daughter—you inherit the family business.

"I'm sorry, I meant the second one on that page, Number Forty-Three. Just that measure, ten times, please. That will get it solidly in your fingers." I hate that piece. Sixteenth notes kill me. On the other hand, if I could just *sing* it . . .

"Again."

"Again, please."

"Again."

He stands to the side of the window as though he doesn't want to be seen.

The sunset casts a pink-gold veil over everything. The music on the stand in front of me is illuminated, and I fall in love with the light, the alto clef curlicuing around the cloudy patterns from Papa's pipe. I may have to suffer through these lessons before I can go off and practice my arias, but I never get tired of being with him.

There is shouting in the street. There's always shouting. Men sound just like their frenzied dogs. There are five gunshots, and my bow bounces on the strings as I flinch.

Papa, almost imperceptibly, closes the curtains, staying behind them. He turns to me with something like panic in his eyes, though he is smiling.

"Gerta, why don't you try it again on my viola instead." Mine is just the French practice instrument Papa himself learned to play on as a child. He takes it from me and lays the priceless Guarneri on the table. I pick up the precious viola and play the étude again, watching him rummage through cabinets and drawers. He has a handful of packages of rosin, all that he can find, and he packs them into the compartment in the good case, along with a few envelopes of extra strings and a spare tuning peg, as though he were trying to cram every bit of viola paraphernalia into that one case. He removes it all again, repacks it, again, again.

"Papa?" I have stopped my scales and am just staring at him, the bow and viola hanging at my side. The pipe is trembling in his mouth. He looks at me quickly, in the middle of re-coiling a D string. He stands up straight and draws a slow breath.

"We can stop for tonight, *Liebchen*. You did well." He takes the instrument from me and places it in the case. Through a sliver in the curtains, I see that the sunset has faded now to purple, and the first star appears in the sky.

Maria comes out of the kitchen, wiping her hands on her apron. She withdraws her big emerald ring from the apron pocket and puts it on her middle finger. She glances at the stuffed case, exchanges a look with my father that

I cannot read—worry? Are they angry with me? Were my scales that bad?

"Come with me, Gertalein," she says, and I follow her into her bedroom, which smells of powdery roses and that musky smell grown-ups give off when they sleep. She rifles through her closet: the turquoise silk blouse with red buttons, the pale pink flowered dress with a ruffled hem.

"What do you like in here, darling?"

"What do you mean? I like everything!" I say, sitting on the edge of the bed.

"I mean, I'd like to give you something pretty. I was going to donate some clothes to the war effort and thought I'd give you the first choice before I do."

I have always coveted Maria's clothes. There was one night when she and Papa were away—she'll never know about it—I had my own private fashion show in her room. I tried on everything, including every single shade of lipstick. I felt guilty about that for weeks. And now she is offering me *anything* I want.

"Really?"

"Yes, whatever you'd like."

I run my hand over the soft silks and cashmeres, and choose a pink blouse with red roses, and a grass-colored cardigan to go over it.

Maria pulls out a gown the same color as her green eyes, with tiny crystals on the bodice. It is just like the dress I used to picture as a little girl, when I imagined myself a famous singer.

"Gerta, how about this one? For your debut."

"To *keep*?" My eyes are so wide, they forget how to blink.

"Yes, of course! You have to start as you mean to go on, dear. You have a long life of concert gowns ahead of you."

"Oh, Maria. Thank you. I won't let anything happen to it."

"Just wear it in good health, my love. Here, let's hang it up in your room." She hangs the gown on my closet door, and I lay the blouse and sweater over my desk chair. Then she hugs me—not an average good-night pat, but a complete and total embrace.

CHAPTER 11

Everyone is obsessed with blood, with who your parents are, your grand-parents—fractions of fractions. Surveys are taken in schools, but since I'm tutored at home, we don't have to deal with such things. People everywhere wear yellow stars on their coat sleeves, even on their best dresses. We don't, of course, because we're *Germans*.

Maria does all of the errands. Papa has some private students but only plays in the orchestra if someone's sick. He has moved from first to last chair in his section. I think he takes his boredom out on me—my viola lessons grow more intense. Still, I'm just a passable player—but I'm going to *sing* every moment I can. I even hum the viola parts as I glide the bow across the strings. Though I only practice with the children's choir once a month now, Maria still speaks enthusiastically of my debut, which is to be at the mid-summer festival.

It is the seventeenth of June; my alarm clock ticks 2:00, 2:30 a.m. Tomor-row is an important rehearsal of the *St. Matthew Passion*. I finally fall asleep and dream of the Greek Titans in my school lesson, battling to a backdrop of thundering bass in "Da qual tremore insolito" from *Don Giovanni.* In reality, the pounding is of fists on the front door, and I bolt awake. There are soldiers inside the apartment, turning over chairs, ransacking drawers. Maria is waxing indignant about the intrusion and demanding that they leave. Papa rushes into my room and tells me to dress quickly and pack a bag. His is already packed. He must have been expecting this; he is even wearing his hat.

I open my nightstand drawer and grab a stack of photographs, the Wohlfahrt études and the music for my debut and put them in Papa's viola case. I shove Maria's pink blouse and some other clothes into my weekend bag and throw on the green sweater. Something tells me to bring my snack stash as well. We are hurried down the stairs and marched down Hofstrasse toward the Residenz square. I carry the viola case, and Papa carries both of our bags. Maria stands in the doorway in her robe, holding her shawl across her mouth, saying nothing in protest. Why doesn't she run after us? Why isn't she coming, too?

The orange trees lining the square are in full fragrance, almost sickly sweet in the balmy night air, which is sticky with the barking of the SS.

"You Jews are no longer . . . safe . . . here in Würzburg. We are taking you into protective custody and moving you to the east, where you will be resettled."

What? Who are they talking about? Am I still dreaming?

People start shouting out questions to the soldiers. "What about my house? I didn't have time to get the deed out of the safe." "I need to tell my tenants where to send their rent." "I need to go to the bank, to my safe-deposit box, to my—"

The head officer's voice becomes a little softer when he realizes that he is losing order.

"Now, now, there's nothing to worry about. Why don't you each write down your concerns on a little slip of paper, and we will make sure to hand

them over to the proper channels. We are simply escorting you to the station. Stay close together, now. Parents, mind your children. Look at the poor dears, so sleepy. You'll be able to ask your questions when we get there. Not to worry."

Papa grasps my hand. I look in his eyes. I don't like what I see there. He obviously wants to tell me something but dares not.

This is not a mistake after all, is it?

CHAPTER 12

On the fifteen-minute walk to the Würzburg station, the young soldiers can't decide whether to treat us like humans or dogs. The tone changes from minute to minute. Würzburg isn't a big town; somehow they must remember that we're their *neighbors*. The baker whose pillowy, plummy Buchtel rolls were voted Bavaria's best. The only honest mechanic in town. Papa's friend, the novelist who lives above the tavern. That soldier by the Residenz gate is the one we've passed every day for years. But as quickly as the recognition registers, a steel door slides over the soldiers' faces and we are . . . a herd of goats.

Thirty minutes before, I was in my soft bed, dreaming in music. My debut aria, "Erbarme dich," is still in my throat, caught there just at the surface like ice in water. There's still sleep dust in my eyes, the crease of the pillowcase on my skin. I clutch the handle of the viola case with one hand, and Papa's hand with the other. We are hoisted up into a train car—not one for people, with padded seats and windows and a view of the passing countryside. This is the kind cattle are transported in—a dark wooden crate with the barest slits for ventilation, the cars linked so long that I can't see the engine or the caboose. They shove us in. It takes everything within the parents' control to keep hold of their children and babies.

The promised opportunity to ask our questions is denied. Men and women wave their little slips of paper in the soldiers' faces until the wind snatches them, fluttering the requests away like a summer snow. Once we are in the train, there are no more words between soldiers and passengers. There are only one-way petitions: "Where are we going?" "I want to talk to my lawyer! This can't be legal!" "When are we coming back?" "Can't I get a message to my neighbor to check in on the cat? I'll just be a minute!" "My daughter, she's at a friend's in Frankfurt and won't know I'm gone—" *"But I don't want to leave. I live here."*

Once the train starts to roll, my father tells me everything.

"Gertalein," he whispers, "what do you remember about your mother?"

"Little things," I whisper back, perplexed. I don't think of her much, and I feel terrible for that. I was old enough to remember her more than I do. But for some reason, there's a brick wall whenever I try to call up a memory of my mother.

"What kinds of things?"

"She painted little watercolors. She had dark blond hair."

He purses his lips, nods slowly, looks off into an invisible space. "Do you remember when we left Köln?"

"Yes, Papa. I remember leaving in the night, in the car. There was fire everywhere."

"Yes, Gerta. That was a terrible night. We called it the Night of Broken

Glass. To tell you the truth, I was glad to leave. To me, Köln will always be the place I lost your mother."

"You've never spoken of her since then, Papa."

"I know. I hoped we could leave it all behind. I worked very hard to create a new story for us."

"Tell me about her." Sweat is rolling down my back, and I take off the cardigan, stuffing it into the bag between my feet. Babies take turns wailing.

"We were artists, Gerta. We believed in beauty, truth. We wanted to pull heaven down to earth. We had many friends, went to many parties—we were part of a club. A Jewish club."

He looks me in the eye with an intensity that makes my head throb.

"Jewish?" My eyes don't know where to focus.

"Yes, my love."

"But . . . how could we be? We're not religious. What are you talking about?"

"Gerta, when you were just a little girl, they passed laws. They put a definition on everyone—who was German, who was not. Who was 'Aryan,' and especially who was a Jew. Who was human, who was . . . well. This was

all meaningless, you understand—both of our families had been in Germany for generations. But people will believe anything, about anyone, in the right packaging." He tilts his head back and fishes for a deep breath of the stagnant air above our heads.

"Your mother sensed before I did that things were going to get bad. We had already been planning to leave Köln and start somewhere else—maybe

France, England—change our names, live quietly until Hitler was gone. We thought, *This cannot go on. Surely people will realize they are being fed lies.* But madness had infected Germany and seeped into the national mind. And before we could leave, she . . ."

"Oh, Papa."

"You weren't even four. After the election, things happened so fast. Your mother was part of a political movement. She wanted to try to slow things down, to try to make people come back to reason, but no one could stay ahead of the rapid changes. So, you see, she was at a meeting at the Jewish club, and there was a raid. She was trying to push her way through the chaos to get back to us.

"I was home with you that night, and you were already tucked into bed. My friend Reinhart was there. We were drinking whiskey. My brother Bernard showed up in a panic, and I left you with Reinhart. When Bernard and I reached your mother, it was too late. I recognized her yellow dress, the freckle on her arm." Papa's chin is shaking. In the compressed mass of people, I find his hand and squeeze it. "We buried her quickly, Gerta. We had to. But before we did, I kissed her hand . . . and slipped off her wedding ring." He dissolves.

The train lurches and an involuntary cry goes up from the whole carload trying to keep their balance.

Hours pass. Papa has fallen asleep, tear stains crystallized on his face. I drowse from the exhaustion of holding myself up on the jerking train. I dream I am lying in the backseat of a car, my head on Papa's lap, watching the moon follow us. It glows on Papa's face. He holds his fist to his mouth and clenches his jaw again, again.

"Gerta!" he whispers sharply, stirring me awake. "Gertalein, I have to finish. I do not know what will happen next."

"All right, Papa." I am so thirsty, I can barely swallow.

"I took your mother's wedding ring to the viola maker. He was in the Resistance. He had a steady hand, and he knew how to forge identification papers, the *Ahnenpass*. I . . . sold the ring to him. He made us *Richter*, Gerta. But our name is *Rausch*."

"Rausch." I speak the name, which tastes unfamiliar in my mouth.

"You and I lived our quiet lives in Köln for a few more years. But we were squeezed from every side. I simply wanted to keep things normal for you. I didn't have your mother's foresight or her strategic mind. By then, it was too late to leave Germany.

"The night of the riots, when you were nine, the beautiful old synagogue was burned to the ground. Any shop owned by a Jew was looted and destroyed. Old men were beaten, women were pulled out into the street by their hair, homes were robbed by our own neighbors. The police stood by and did nothing, or laughed, or helped.

"Maria Büchner was my friend through orchestral circles. Musicians look out for each other, you know. I phoned her immediately, and Reinhart risked his life to drive us all the way to Würzburg. Town after town was on fire, all over the country. Maria took us in that very night. When anyone asked, she told them I was just her friend Klemens from conservatory. Anything she decided to do was seen as one of her many charming aspects. So what, if she wanted to take in a gentleman and his daughter—who needed to know more? And we had a few good years, didn't we, Gerta?" He gives an exhausted smile.

"I love our life," I say. Then there is a question I never thought to ask. "Papa, do you . . . love her? The way you loved my mother?"

"It's a different kind. But yes, Gerta, I do. I would have married her, if it wouldn't have raised too many questions. And she loves you, too, like her own daughter."

The train whistle blows. Hardly anyone speaks now. An old woman near the corner begins to moan and mutter. A sweaty toddler lifts up a kitten-like wail for water. The interminable length of train cars carries a miserably bowed drone across the rhythm of the tracks.

"All of this," I say, "is why I couldn't go to school?"

"Yes, and why we rarely left the house. I tried to fade into the background in the orchestra. In the end, it became too dangerous for me to go out at all, and I kept only the few students I felt I could trust."

"Like me." I manage a smile.

"Like you," he says. "Though I would not call you an anointed player." He winks and we laugh. His eyes are like distant stars. "But I was desperate to share my music with you, Gertalein. It has always been the language I speak best. No, more than that. I thought I could hide you in music, like Moses in the basket. I felt the time growing short."

"Those people we saw being marched out of town . . ."

"Jews, like us. I knew they would eventually come for us, but I thought—how foolish—I thought maybe because you were a child, they wouldn't take you, that you could take my viola and your beautiful voice and carry on with your life."

Papa rubs his face. "A father's dream," he whispers. "A father's dream."

CHAPTER 13

The train thrusts forward, drawing out the weak screams of the still conscious. There's a little girl next to me, bobbed mousy brown hair, strawberries on her dress collar. She has a tiny stuffed-animal puppy tucked into that collar, right under her chin. She's standing over the body of her mother, whom she can't get to wake up. She is crying so loudly. I'm paralyzed.

The train door slides open for the first time in days, and we are hurried out. It's a long way down to the ground. The train is so close to the depot building, we can barely stand together. The sign on the yellow wall says BAHNHOF THERESIENSTADT.

An SS guard comes to us and pins a piece of colored paper on our shirts. "Name."

"Klemens and Gerta Richter," says Papa, handing him our papers.

"No *Richter* here on the list." The guard looks at us suspiciously. "Is that your real name? Oh, wait, I do see a Klemens and Gerta here, but it's *Rausch*. Nice try," he says with a smirk. "Occupation?"

Papa sighs. "Violist with the Würzburg Orchestra."

"Ah yes, the Würzburg transport. A real music town, isn't it? Theresienstadt's the place for you, then. Lots of uppity artists."

There are strangers going through our bags. I want to shout at them, but the number of guns hinting in our direction makes me think it's better to stay quiet. Thankfully, Papa still has his viola in his hand. A man tries to grab it, but Papa resists.

"Pay him if you want to keep your instrument," says the guard.

"What?"

"Pay the man, *Schwein*!" he spits. Papa reaches for a few coins in his pocket and hands them to the thief, who looks at him in disgust and walks away.

"From now on, pay in bread," says the guard pragmatically. "How old is the girl?"

"Sixteen," Papa lies. I can't help shooting him a quick look before I realize what he's doing. The guard escorts us to the registration table.

"Musicians' building for him, girls' building L410 for her," the guard tells the registrar while lighting a cigarette. As he walks away, he throws the match at Papa, and it singes a hole in his shirt. The registrar gives us our papers and a card with a grid of tear-off numbers. It looks like some kind of game.

"Ration tickets," she says. "Don't lose these; you won't get more until next month."

The guards are shouting to everyone to report to their quarters. Confusion reigns. Papa takes out a pen and writes his building number on my hand: *B4, Hannover*.

"Write this down somewhere safe. I'll find you. Don't worry, Gertalein.

It's not a big town. Look over there—there's a lady pushing her baby in a stroller. It can't be so bad. Maybe you'll meet some girls your age."

He's shuffled away with a huge cohort of men, and I am separated from Papa for the first time in my life.

This town would actually be pretty if it weren't so chaotic, with soldiers and guns and these massive crowds everywhere. For a minute, the sound becomes so overwhelming that my brain flips a switch and somehow all goes quiet. I look around at the rows of orderly buildings. It looks as though everything here were built in one day, in the same quaint time as the Residenz palace back home, just smaller. Everything is so *right*. The houses look like they were painted in sorbet—cream, minty green, mustard yellow and pretty salmon pink. If I didn't know better, I'd think the whole town was decorated for a summer luncheon.

The sun has gone down over the rampart walls, and the guards manning them turn into silhouettes. Just when I'm thinking that maybe this won't be so bad as long as I can lie down in a bed, I notice how dark the town is. There are street lamps but hardly any lights on in the many, many windows that looked so picturesque just a little while before. But it's not only the lamps that aren't lit. It's hard to describe. There's just no *light* here.

I'm bumbling through the street, stunned. I'm surrounded by several girls my age—I'm not sure at which point I was filtered down into this group—led by a *Kapo*, an old woman in a uniform jacket with a kerchief over her furrowed brow. She ushers us through a heavy arched wooden entryway, through an empty courtyard and up the stairs to a door. It looks like a storage closet, just one bare lightbulb glowing over shelves of suitcases. There's a stench coming out of the room, like sweat and pee and that vinegary smell of fresh vomit. There are voices in there. It sounds like a *lot* of people. What are they all doing in a closet?

"Why are you just standing there staring, you little bitches? Find a bed!"

"A bed?" I ask. "Where?" The woman sucks her teeth and marches down the hall, her heels smacking on the tile floor. I look closer—what I took to be closet shelves are just the front layer of a complex construction. The shelves are in fact the ends of wooden bunk beds, three tiers high, seven beds deep. I quickly do the math. There are more than eighty beds in this room the size of Maria's sitting room at home. Somehow the twelve of us in my group have to find a space in here.

My head is spinning. How long has it been since I've eaten? A girl with jet-black braids locks eyes with me and waves me over. "There's a free bed here," she says. I sit down on a bottom bunk. The bed above is too low for me to sit up straight. I hunch and open my bag, exhausted and trembling. The box of crackers I had been rationing is missing. So is the little bag of hard candies—almost everything is gone but an old dress and a pair of underwear. I'm hungry and confused and I just want my papa. What is happening? What *is* this place?

"You'll want to shake out the linens first," the girl says. "They were supposed to disinfect in here weeks ago. Don't worry. The bedbugs are itchy, but you get used to it." I should care about this, but I'm so overwhelmed, I just clutch my bag to my chest and pass out.

Crack!

"Aufwachen!"

I sit up and smack the top of my head on the bunk above me. It's all too true: I really am here in this place.

A whistle blows outside our building.

"*Schnell, schnell!*" shouts the *Kapo* from yesterday. We're herded into line to get our first bread ration, but one of the girls from my transport is late coming out. A guard waves her over. With a robotic movement of his arm, he simply shoots her between the eyes, spattering her blood all over our bread. A thick numbness rolls through me.

ONE, two, three, four, five, six, seven, eight-and-ONE, two, three, four . . .

Instantly I begin counting a beat in my head, automating my actions. My brain simply takes over the responsibility of making sure I'm in lockstep, and I become as mechanical as the guard. This is the first murder I've ever witnessed, and I understand perfectly that it won't be my last. Now I see the buildings in a different light. The paint is peeling off their gray concrete walls. The charm and order are an obscenity.

After our paltry breakfast, I'm called with the other newcomers to a table where the old woman gives us work assignments. I'm to work at the clothing shop. She waves another girl over. I recognize her; she's from my room, actually. She's tall and very pretty, and I can tell she's rich.

"Roza! Take her to the shop with you and get her up to speed."

"Come on," says Roza impatiently, tossing her honey-colored hair. The clothing shop is just catty-corner to our barracks. It's airless and hot inside and musty, like dirty laundry. On my mostly empty stomach, the odor makes me instantly nauseous.

"It's not hard, okay?" she huffs. "You have to sort the clothes in this pile into the right categories and hang them up by size. Think you can get that?"

"Sure," I say. I have a vested interest in getting things right; the image of the girl being shot keeps flashing through my mind.

On a shelf behind the counter is a basket of yellow stars and spools of thread. Jewelry lines the glass display case—nothing of value, just cheap-looking costume pieces—along with used lipsticks and half-empty bottles of shaving lotion.

A customer comes in looking for underwear and socks. Roza turns on some charm and persuades her to buy a pair of shoes, too. She takes the fellow prisoner's combined currency of camp money, ration tickets and an additional "tip" for the shoes—two cigarettes wrapped in a bit of newspaper. As I'm sorting, I spot something familiar, but I don't say anything. It's a pink blouse with red roses on it. And there's Maria's green cardigan. I grab them; they still smell like her gardenia perfume.

"Roza," I whisper after the customer leaves, "these are my clothes!"

"Of course they are, stupid. These are all our clothes. Right down to the underwear. If you like it that much, you can always buy it back. You'll just have to go without food for a couple days. Want it now? Or should I put it on lay-away for you?" She laughs. Roza's brand of cruelty is new to me.

The next customer comes in, and Roza shows her *my* clothes on purpose, going on and on about how perfectly suited they are to this woman's coloring, and makes the sale.

I haven't seen Papa in a week, and I'm starting to panic. I step out of the hellish clothing shop, and a girl hands me a flyer for a concert in the café on the town square. It's starting in ten minutes. The strange thing about this café, I realize, is that there doesn't seem to be any food or any actual *coffee*— just weak, bitter tea ladled from a big stockpot. I take a cup and am trying to find a table when someone grabs my arm—

Papa!

We cling to each other until my breath gives out. He looks awful, unshaven and tired. But we sit down, hoping that some music will reset our hearts. It's a nice concert, in fact. It seems out of place here among the hideousness, but the players are world-class, Papa says. He leans over to me.

"That's Albert," he whispers, "the conductor. I played with him in conservatory. I haven't seen him in fifteen years. Imagine."

Then something surprising happens: *Roza* takes the stage. She plays a few pieces from Schumann's *Kinderszenen*. Just the easy ones. Even *I* can play those, and piano is my third instrument. Her playing is as wooden as that of any average girl who takes her lessons once a week. But after the concert, Roza is swarmed by girls, and more than a few boys. She's obviously popular here and knows it. Papa goes to talk with his conductor friend and comes back to the table, beaming.

"Albert says I can join the orchestra!" he says. "That means I can get out of the job they gave me."

"What job were you doing?"

"Never mind that, *Liebchen*. This is a good turn of fortune. Music to the rescue, right?"

It doesn't change anything for me; I still have to work in the shop with Roza. But Papa and I share the viola, and before curfew every day he drills me in my études and I improve. I even get to perform a little chamber music. But I wish I could find a way to *sing*. I feel like if I could work on an aria, I could shed some of this nervous energy building up alongside my gnawing hunger.

The reality of life here becomes clear very fast. It's filthy, crowded; dead bodies lie stacked in horse-drawn carts in the street; people are shot or beaten for no reason—but inexplicably, there are concerts and plays. I don't know if it's a mercy or part of a big, cruel Nazi game.

A Sunday concert is just letting out, and some of the kids are trading pieces on the grand piano. They practically beg Roza to perform, and she sets to it, all talk and no substance. I can't take it anymore. Roza's bragging and the way she makes life so unbearable at the clothing shop drive me to do it. I take a deep breath, so deep it feels like my diaphragm hits my knees, and sing the highest note I can at full voice. All the kids turn around, stunned.

From that point on, Roza is more subdued. The girls in our room want to know where I learned to sing like that and what I'm going to do when we get out of this nightmare.

"Be a famous mezzo, of course," I say.

But at the shop, if I let my guard down for a minute, I'll turn around to find all the clothes I've just folded knocked to the floor.

CHAPTER 14

We've been in this prison-town for almost a year, but something is changing. All week, there's been a film crew here, and we're reassigned from our normal jobs to spruce things up, planting flowers, painting buildings, clearing out beds. For some reason, trains are leaving more frequently, resettling people farther east. It's nice to have some more space, but it means a lot of tearful goodbyes.

Children are taught new songs to sing together. We teenagers are given extra camp money to spend in the store on makeup and clean, if threadbare, dresses. Of course, we have to ruin them with the yellow star. Even after a year of living in Theresienstadt, I'm not used to it. We are instructed in new protocols and shown the consequences of not playing along.

"The Red Cross is coming to pay us a visit," says the commandant in a tone dripping with innuendo. "Let's show them the best face of our little town, shall we?"

Roza, naturally, has to have a lead role. She's still strutting, even though the circles under her eyes are getting darker. The film crew can't get enough of her playing her little piano pieces, as though she were some prodigy. If only they'd get a close-up, they'd see her hair crawling with lice, just like the rest of ours.

But I, too, have friends here now. And it's a good week for us. There's more to eat. We're giving concerts and plays several times a day. There are soccer games, and the mothers are allowed to bring out all the babies for us to play with.

The film crew packs up and leaves Theresienstadt to put their movie together for God knows what. No sooner does the exhaust from their trucks clear the air than the commandant starts shouting. A roll is called, and the block guards rush us to the town square. Some of the girls in my block are here, but not Roza. I suppose they want to keep her around to show off to the Red Cross.

Papa comes running out from the café building, pulling on his suit jacket, when a very young guard, for fun, sticks his foot out and sends him sprawling toward the edge of a brick half wall. I hear the bone in his leg crack against it. The guard is red-faced with laughter. Somehow Papa manages to get himself in line. To stay on the ground would be unthinkable here.

"The camp is getting overcrowded," the commandant begins with a sharp look at the laughing guard, "and we need to give the Red Cross a good impression. Some of you will be moved farther east and resettled on farms." He begins this selection by sneeringly calling my father out to head the line. A few more people get into their ranks, and Papa motions to me to join him once it seems safe to do so. And so we have five minutes in which to pack our bags and board the train for these farms in the east.

Albert tells Papa that he'll pack his bag for him, and I run back to my barracks to grab my things. We meet near the square and help Papa to the train platform down the street. Albert has a stash of pain pills and a bottle of tea for Papa. Papa is sweating, tears running down his face, but he is completely silent. There's something in his eyes that I've never seen before: terror. On the transport here to Theresienstadt, there had been urgency, even some fear, but not like this. My strong papa. My gentle father—an artist, so uncompromised in his own peace—looks like a terrified, wounded animal now.

And he will not say a word to me.

CHAPTER 15

I see three sunrises and sunsets on the train from Theresienstadt. The May weather is still cool outside, but inside this train car it is stifling. Most of us carry little or nothing, but I have Papa's viola. I won't let it be lost or trampled. As long as we have this music between us, we are a family.

Papa is delirious with pain. He is unable to bear the standing and squeezing. Mercifully, we are able to maneuver to the car wall, and he sinks down, passing out instantly.

The train screeches, slows, whines. The clacking tempo decreases until we stop. A rush of wind blows through the two small windows. It smells of a sweetish smoke. It is not wood smoke.

I help Papa to his feet and let him lean on my shoulder. The car doors are flung open, and we are herded out, with brown dogs barking at us. Papa falls to the ground, and a dog gets right in his face, red-gummed and yellow-toothed. I put Papa's arm around my neck and hoist him to standing again.

"Are you all right, Papa? Just hold on to me."

"Gerta—Gerta—" This is all he can manage through the pain, and he is holding me so tight, it hurts; he is stroking my face and hair, not tenderly, but rather as though trying to imprint me on his own skin.

"Papa, what's happening? Where are we?"

At the far end of the train is a man with a baton, a conductor. To the side, behind the barbed wire, a small group of women plays in some kind of orchestra. They are playing Mozart, but with a weird, dissonant arrangement of mandolins, accordions and a snare drum.

He is not conducting *them*, but *us*.

We are pushed forward into a mass, which he is dividing into two lines.

Clutching the viola case, I arrive at the conductor. His eyes are dark. He is smiling, whistling through a gap in his teeth. He stops his conducting and taps my case with his baton. The dogs are still barking.

"Ah!" he says. "A musician! Violin? No, of course, viola. Yes, you, go over there, and the *Kapo* will take your information. You'll be an asset. Viola. Not so common."

"But it's not my—" I start to say.

"Next!" says the conductor. "To the right. To the left. *Da da dee, da dee dum . . .*"

As I am hurried on, I turn to look for my father. He is in the other line. He is limping on his broken leg, staring desperately at me, openmouthed, like he needs to tell me something. The others in the line with him are mostly women with babies, little children, old men—and cripples. Like a stream running down into the ocean, the line veers toward a distant fog, out of which rises a tall, smoking chimney.

I am led to a room with countless other women. None of them are the ones with children. We are told to give our occupations or skills to the registrar.

"Chemist."

"Nurse."

"Musician," I say, holding up the viola case. I wonder what questions they are asking Papa right now, and I wish there were a way to get his instrument back to him.

"I see," says the registrar. "And were you sent here because of that?"

"Yes, the conductor told me to come here."

She chuckles. "The 'conductor.' Ah. I see. He must have liked the look of you." She finishes filling out my card. "Take this to the next room. Tell them 'Women's Orchestra.'"

I try to be cheerful, hoping a good demeanor will make it go well for me.

"Thank you very much, ma'am," I say compliantly. I go into the next room and stop short in the doorway. Women sit on benches as men walk down the rows. Some have huge scissors; some have electric clippers. They are shaving the heads of the women, who cry hot tears. Another man follows the barbers, carrying a small, battered toolbox full of needles and metal attachments.

I am shoved onto a bench, and I quickly slide the viola case between my feet. The man with the clippers grabs my thick chestnut hair, twists it into a clump, pulls a pair of scissors out of his pocket and cuts the whole of it off.

"Lice," he says dully. "It's bad here." The next man follows with the clippers and shaves my head clean in five quick passes. I can't even process what's happening to me.

The other man comes with his tool kit. He presses a needle into the soft, thin skin inside my left forearm and sloppily tattoos a number: *A28865*. I feel every nerve in my arm connect to some other part of my body, and electricity is shooting through all of me, making me sweat instantly. He writes the number on my card and tells me to show it to the guard. I almost forget the viola. I grab it just in time, before someone else takes my place on the bench.

A fat woman, chewing on her cheek and twirling a lanyard of keys, gives me a striped uniform and tells me to strip and to leave my old clothes on the stool. I take off my Theresienstadt dress, and it rubs against the raw wound of the tattoo, shooting a twinge to the top of my head. I know what this change of uniform means; every so often I had been told in the other camp that my clothes would be laundered, disinfected and returned to me. I never saw them after that. For months, I've worn that threadbare dress, and part of me is glad to be rid of it. But these blue-and-gray-striped pants and shirt take from me the last distinction.

I am genderless—a shaved, numbered and striped inmate.

The guard looks at my card and directs me to the entrance to the women's camp. In the distance, near the massive brick gateway, I can see that the train has been emptied. The musicians are hastily packing up their instruments. Something feels different: I hear none of the usual post-performance chatter, nothing about botched notes or particularly sublime passages.

That congratulatory conversation is occurring instead among the laughing guards while their dogs lie on the ground, finally quieted, chewing bones.

Blood coagulates on the ground, and to the side I see about eight or ten inmates hauling bodies into the back of a truck. Some of the dead wear striped uniforms like mine. Some are still in street clothes. There are children among them. Babies. Little boys in knee socks. Their hats fall off their heads as they are picked up and hurled roughly into the truck bed. I want my papa.

Someone shouts at me. "You! With the instrument! Get back over to the musicians. There's nothing to look at here." I feel an arm around me. I hadn't known anyone was near.

"Come with me," the woman says softly, pragmatically. "You've been sent to the orchestra, yes? Well. Join your very lucky sisters. Music has saved your life today."

"Where's my papa?" I plead with her. "I want my papa!"

She sighs and points ahead. "See that chimney?" she says, still softly, but so that I will clearly understand. "See that smoke? There's your papa."

CHAPTER 16

Maybe it's July. Maybe August; I've stopped keeping track. The air is suffocating. There are no trees to give shelter overhead, only the forest hedging the camp. Cicadas mercilessly rattle in the branches of that faraway shade.

Our director lifts her baton. From the first note—relief. I can't hear the insects. I can't smell the smoke. I pour myself down the horsehair of the bow.

My hands have become my father's hands.

I know what happened to him now. His broken leg made the decision for him. I've watched his death daily, as the Women's Orchestra provides an artifice of calm and succor to the passengers being unloaded and sorted. They become two rivers: one flowing right, to the shave-tattoo-uniform; one flowing left, to the chimney, evaporating into the air we breathe, raining into the mud we walk in. And the conductor, Mengele, stands at the fork of these two rivers, keeping time to the music we provide him.

We can say nothing, do nothing. In the beginning, I would try to send messages with my eyes to the people in the line, pleading with that grandmother to throw aside her cane and straighten her spine at all costs, to that skinny boy to put on the strongest, most robust persona he could muster. *"Arbeit macht frei,"* I would will, *if only for a few months. Just live a few more months.*

After a while, my understanding changed. Now I lower my eyes. Every one of us who comes through that gate is damned to the same fate, ultimately. We can't escape; we can't change a thing. But, I think, we can provide peace to the mothers and the babies on that long walk in the last few minutes of their lives. That has to be some kind of mercy. I have to believe that, because plenty of prisoners spit at us as traitors. They hate us because, like the Jews of the *Sonderkommando,* who shove the dead into the ovens, we earn our extra bread by being part of the machine that kills their children. How do I answer this charge? I play, as sweetly as I can. I play like Papa did.

I will always see the snow falling thick on a mother marching toward the chimney with a baby on her breast. She is unfazed by the cold on her skin, unapologetic for soothing her infant and herself. Two laughing officers snatch the baby from her nipple and dash it, still swallowing milk, against the train wheel. They push her against the car, ripping and tearing not just her clothes. She crumples next to her child, both writhing in the snow until two bullets join them in death.

As I lie on the hard wood and dirty straw of my bunk, I think about the night the angel came to me, giving me my new voice. That was the first time I thought about God. As my body rounded and my voice deepened, I was struck by this mysterious question of *why. Why* is music? And *why* do girls have to stumble across these invisible lines to become women?

I began to sing to the questions, and they sang back not answers, but more questions. There was a rhythm that started coursing through my body like an electric current, and I developed a habit of doing everything to a count of eight so I could make music out of these new, confusing feelings.

The music, the rhythm, the vibration of light in my joints and marrow somehow continue, even here in Auschwitz. I learn to stay just under the surface, doing everything to the eight-count. I blend like dust into dust, complying, a brick in the architecture.

As exhausted, hungry families disembark from the trains, I silence the *why* of my complicity. I think, *If I fold into a small ball of patience, surely things can't get any worse.*

CHAPTER 17

The first of November comes to Auschwitz with early rushes of snow and wind. The block guard turns on the weak light and bangs her club on the bunks to wake us. We spring up and dress, throwing our blankets over our bald heads and shoving our feet into the wrong shoes. We grab our instruments, thinking it's time to play for a late transport or a midnight work detail. She hurries us out into the night air, which instantly freezes the tears in our tired eyes. We run toward the tracks, but instead of gathering on the sidelines, we are shoved into the waiting cattle car ourselves. The fifty of us fill a car. *Not again*, I think.

We're not packed as tightly as we were upon our arrival, but it's ironic— now I wish for that closeness to insulate me from the icy air blowing in. We huddle together in a corner. The straw is filthy and has obviously not been changed for many transports. Even after the *Sonderkommando* revolted a few weeks ago and destroyed one of the crematoria, three of the chimneys visible through the open train door are still glowing red, the smoke pluming pale against the dark sky.

The guard tosses in a few loaves of stale bread and a bucket of water and slides the door shut, its steel pin dropping into place. A minute later, we are moving. We are so resigned to the nearness of our deaths that the question simply becomes, *Is it today?* There's no crying, no panic. There is only silence, and cold.

This song begins softly from the lips of a cellist:

> *Az ir vet, kinderlekh, elter vern, vet ir aleyn farshteyn—*
> When, dear children, you grow older, you will understand
>   for yourselves—

I can see the notes hanging on her frozen breath. Some others know the melody, a few words, and add harmonies. We feel a bit warmer, enough to take out our instruments and join in. We play to the rhythm of the clacking wheels on the tracks—*ba-dumm ba-dumm, two three, ba-dumm ba-dumm, two three*. We do some pieces from our repertoire and, now that we're alone, some forbidden composers, too. I swear I can smell Maria's gardenia perfume.

There are endless mornings and evenings. We arrive at Bergen-Belsen.

III

FAST FRIENDS

Bergen-Belsen Displaced Persons Camp

Summer–Fall 1945

CHAPTER 18

I didn't know until Lev told me: there are four words in Hebrew that mean "world," and one of them means "hidden world." He says that in each of us is a hidden world. Each of us *is* a world. Each baby born, a world created, a possibility. Each one who dies, a red star smoldering out. And in all of this, the hidden places within another person are concealed from us.

Lev and I have become fast friends. It's amazing that after so long here, we all seem new to each other. Just a few months ago, when the British came, everyone was dying. No one really spoke then. Who would bother striking up a conversation you might not live to finish? And what would you say? Everyone had seen the same things. After you've witnessed your twentieth, hundredth, thousandth person perish, words are meaningless. Your life becomes bread. Rainwater. Numbers. Keeping your feet clean. Any obsessive ritual to keep your own heart beating.

But Lev broke the silence.

We walk from lunch every day to this little copse of birch, where we can get away from the camp noise and talk. He tells me about God; I tell him about music—the mysteries of each other's worlds.

Lev sits on the ground, I on a tree stump. He's managed to pull together donated clothes that are more appropriate to his upbringing. The white threads of his tzitzit entwine with the tiny shoots springing up from the base of a tree.

"Lev, before the war, did you just study and pray all the time? I mean, what did you *do*?"

He looks up at me and smiles. "I was an apprentice. At a newspaper."

"Really!"

"Are you surprised?"

"I am. You seem like such a scholar."

"No, not a scholar," he laughs. "There's a newspaper starting here, you know. They just brought in a press. I'm going to join. Know what it's called?"

"What?" I lean in closer, eager to hear.

"*Unzer Sztyme—Our Voice*. Great name, don't you think?"

"*Our Voice*. Yes, it's perfect," I say, meditating for a moment. "That's kind of a commitment, though, isn't it, Lev? Staying to start a newspaper?"

"I know," he says. "I thought we'd have been released by now. I think the British are in over their heads."

We get up and start back to the main square. There's a group of little kids standing in the sunshine, doing hand motions as they sing the Hebrew aleph-bet. Their voices are like chimes in the warming breeze.

"School's in already," says Lev, amused. "Teachers don't waste time, do they?"

"I've got three years of high school to catch up on, myself," I groan.

"Look at their faces"—Lev smiles—"the kids' and the teachers'. They're in heaven."

We stop in the middle of the square at the announcement board that lists jobs and training opportunities. The camp pulsates with this collective energy, gearing up for change. Everyone is hungry to engage their minds and hands.

One advertisement in particular grabs my attention: I sign my name on the list for the new camp musical society.

CHAPTER 19

Auditions are to take place at ten. There are a lot of people in the line, more than I would have expected. Some have their instruments in beat-up cases like mine. Some just hold them—a tarnished flute, a mandolin missing three of eight terribly corroded strings. I'm thankful I still have some rosin left for my bow, but it definitely needs new horsehair. I wonder whether the relief agencies will see value in helping us get these trifles.

"Gerta?" a light voice calls from behind me, and someone touches my shoulder. I turn and see a face I might have known once. Who can tell—no one is the same as they were.

"Roza." She points at herself. "We were in Theresienstadt together . . . ?" I study her through squinted eyes.

"Ah," I say. "Of course. How could I ever forget you." It's not exactly thrilling to see her, but there's a kind of weighty relief in seeing *anyone* with whom I have a history. I put my arms around her, and the viola case hits the back of her shoulder. "You made it. Good. That's good."

"You kept your viola, through all this?" she says. "How in the world?"

"Women's Orchestra. Auschwitz," I say, raising an eyebrow.

"Oh," says Roza.

"How about you?"

"They sent me to Ravensbrück after the Red Cross came. Hard labor."

"Mmm." I nod. "But you're here. Alive. And auditioning?"

"Yes, when I saw them bring in the baby grand, I thought I'd take a chance. I'm really out of practice. A piano, you know"—there's that old smirk again—"not as easy to carry from camp to camp." We have a seat, and I catch a glimpse of her hands folded on her music. Some of her fingers have been broken and healed badly. I remember we used to say she had the hands of a princess.

"Long fingers," she says, noticing my stare, "better for making munitions than playing Mozart, I guess. Oh, but it *is* good to see you, Gerta. You look well."

I laugh sardonically. "It's okay, Roza, you don't have to lie. I can't seem

to gain any weight. Anyway, you must've gotten into the clothing line early. That's a pretty dress."

"Thanks." She smooths the dress self-consciously.

The director is calling us to take our seats in the hall.

"So—I see the viola," Roza whispers. "But please tell me you're going to sing, too. I never got to tell you this—I was a different person then—but I always loved your voice."

This stops me cold. I haven't sung a note since the day we were liberated. I can't. For all the time I've held on to the hope of a singing career, nothing in me wants to utter a note.

"We'll begin with woodwinds, please," says the director. "May I have flutes, clarinets, oboes—I don't suppose we have any bassoons? Ah! But there *is* one! Come up, come up!"

The players assemble together on the stage. Most don't even have an instrument, but the director has several salvaged pieces. He has the musicians tune and do some basic exercises to establish levels of skill. Brass follows next, then percussion.

"Next, strings. May I have my violins, please?"

The violinists are everywhere, at least half the people here. But of course—what respectable family wouldn't have had at least one child playing violin? This must have been why Papa chose the viola instead. He never was one to follow a crowd. A pang of grief hits me. I still feel like he's going to walk through the door any minute.

The violins alone take forty-five minutes, half of which they spend being chatty. If Papa were here, he'd be whispering violist jokes to pass the time.

If you're stranded in the desert, should you look for a good violist, a bad violist or an oasis? A bad violist. The other two are just mirages.

Have you heard the one about the violist who played in tune? Neither have I.

Why shouldn't violists go hiking? Because if they get lost, no one will realize they're gone.

"Cellos, please," says the director. I stir as I realize what a wry smile I'm wearing.

"Double basses," he says next. He is just about to go to percussion when—

"Excuse me, Herr Direktor, violas?" exactly three of us say at the same time, turning midsentence to locate each other, bursting into laughter.

"Of course, of course, I am so sorry! Come, come!" We ascend the stage, and an older player asks me quietly for a bit of rosin.

"My oversight brings up an important point, friends," says the director. "The orchestra would be incomplete without the viola. It is the soul of the orchestra. You may not always be able to discern its sound, but you always know when it is missing."

Roza's audition is rusty, but technique will come with practice, and even with her twisted fingers, she'll find a way, I can tell. She plays with more heart than she used to, and heart can't be taught.

Without the threat of death hanging over us, we finally have the luxury to melt into the music. Afterward, Roza and I walk to dinner, satisfied and smiling.

A few evenings later, Lev and I are sitting in the grove as the first few stars appear through the treetops. He is twirling the long tzitzit from his vest.

"Have you noticed that almost every day now, there's a wedding?" he says. "Crazy, isn't it? All these strangers? A lot of them are really young, too. I saw, the other day, two fifteen-year-olds under the canopy!"

"Hmm, I hadn't noticed," I feign, chewing a slice of apple. "Good for them. But I'm never getting married myself."

"No?"

"No, I'm a musician!" I protest.

"Musicians get married, too, don't they?"

"Well, they have lovers, mostly." I carelessly wave another apple slice in the air. "Several, usually, in different cities."

"Oh, is that right?" he teases.

"Well, what do I know?" I admit, blushing.

"Good luck finding cities full of romance now. I hear they're all in ruins. But lots of people around here seem to be finding love." He looks at me just a little too long. "Or something like it."

"I just think, why risk it? It's foolish." My foot is falling asleep; I get up and walk in a circle.

"Don't you think it's brave, actually?" he suggests.

"Brave? To enter into a contract with someone you hardly know? It's certain failure." I offer him a slice of apple. He smiles and shakes his head.

"All right, then, Gerta the Prophet, if you know the end from the beginning, why go on living at all?"

His directness takes me by surprise. "I—I don't know *why*. You want to live, you don't want to live. What's the alternative, suicide? I don't have it in me."

"You've got to think a bit further forward."

"No, I mean, there's *something* ahead for me. Maybe my voice will come back and I'll be able to go to conservatory. I'm still young enough; my voice wouldn't be mature for another ten years anyway."

"But don't you want a family someday?"

"I'll marry my music." I smile at him with finality.

"But, Gerta"—he is suddenly serious—"why be alone?"

My heart falls a bit. "Because you can lose. You *will* lose. We survived this, but I'll die someday, Lev. You'll die. It might be typhus again, or just crossing the street, or falling off a chair, for God's sake, and hitting your head. It's better to just take care of yourself."

"We all lost someone," says Lev. "We all lost *everyone*. This is going to be a hard enough road. Our parents are dead. Don't you think we all need someone to help us make it through?"

I have no answer to this. I can only think of Maria's advice about men and lipstick and how there's no one left *to* need anymore. No one who really knows me.

"I'm glad you and I are friends, Lev," I say, the tingling in my foot finally subsiding. "I hope you'll get married someday. And have me over for dinner once in a while. Check in on me. Make sure I'm not living backstage under a costume rack somewhere."

"I will make sure of that, Gerta," he says. "You have my word."

There's something attached to the frame of my bed when I lie down this evening. It's a letter from Lev, written on the backs of misprinted forms and wrapped in an envelope fashioned from a sheet of newsprint. The weather has turned brutally cold and damp; even under my two thick blankets, I'm layered in extra clothes and my coat. In my pocket is a hot potato I took from dinner to warm my hands.

Dear Gerta,

How was your day? Congratulations on making the orchestra; I saw your name on the announcement board. It must be good to get back to something familiar.

The newspaper is up and running, and we'll have our first edition out in a few days. The British are going to bring in some English papers to sell, so we're building a proper newsstand as well. It's a relief to read in Yiddish again. For so long, the only things we had to read were German signs and posters, with those awful caricatures of imaginary Jews. This paper may just get different people talking to each other.

I'm finally warming up under the covers, so I kick off my shoes. I unwrap the potato from its wax paper, and it steams its lovely, earthy smell under my nose. I keep a little packet of salt in a shoebox under my bed, and I pinch a bit onto the potato and keep reading.

Anyway, it's good to turn our minds toward tomorrow, isn't it?

Where I came from, my future would have been chosen for me by my mother and father and rabbi, those who knew me best. But they're gone, and we're left to make our own futures. I can only close my eyes and imagine what my father would say to all the questions that run through my mind.

Gerta, I understand your not wanting to get married. Your reasons make sense. They might even protect you. Nothing could be worse than losing everyone we loved. And the sight of you almost dying of the fever haunts me. But you healed, and now you're my friend. There must be better things ahead.

As for me, Gerta, I will get married someday. What they stole from us was not merely our lives, but our ability to choose. I choose to live. And I think you do, too.

But I don't want a girl who clings to me. I want someone who knows
her own mind and speaks it. I want a girl who, despite emerging from hell,
lets herself dream—and helps me to dream again, too.

Lev

The potato is dry and mealy in my mouth. I desperately need water.
Opening my window, I gather some early snow in a cup and chew on it.

CHAPTER 20

Teams of people are in and out of the camp every day. There are groups of men and women walking through with Red Cross armbands. Chaplains visit, too, trying to comfort the hysterical, whose bellies are at last full enough to allow their emotions to surface. Plenty of people have lost themselves completely; as long as they live, they will never stop screaming unless someone holds them very, very tightly.

The chaplains have been trying to reunite survivors, a fruitless effort most of the time. Sometimes they will stand and say Kaddish with those who can muster it. They have religious items for those eager to get back to their old ways. Mostly, though, the chaplains simply sit next to people in silence.

We've been here much longer than we hoped or expected. The British tightly control who leaves and where they relocate. There's a lot of chatter about Palestine, about relatives in America. Almost no one seems to discuss the possibility of going back to their own homes.

I picture myself walking up to the front door of our building and ringing the bell, Maria answering in a silk dress and a cloud of gardenia perfume, laughing with a man who is not my father. *Oh, you lived?* I picture her saying, with that characteristic wave of her hand. *I thought they took care of things when I betrayed you to the SS.*

With that image, any thought I had of going back to Würzburg is crushed to dust.

Everywhere along the main walls of the camp, people post their names. Relief workers bring cameras and take pictures of the children, holding little name signs, now that they have gained enough weight to be recognizable. Their names are sent to registries, but mostly the photographs wave in the wind, unclaimed. Once in a while, one is taken down when a connection is made by a distant relative who remembers: *My cousin had a child by that name.*

In the room I share with twenty other girls, I take Papa's viola case out from under my bed. Inside, under the blue-velvet-covered chipboard, are the tattered photographs and letters I grabbed from my nightstand two years ago. I've stolen countless moments to stare at them:

My parents' wedding portrait, so damaged by water that I can no longer see my mother's face.

Papa performing Mozart's *Sinfonia Concertante*.

My children's choir singing for the queen of the Netherlands.

A tiny watercolor of a peeled orange on a blue-and-white dish, painted by my mother.

Maria before a rapt audience in Berlin, performing her signature aria from *Turandot*.

Me, in the park, six years old, a butterfly resting just below the neckline of my school blouse—when I still went to school.

I could never part with anything from my viola case. Except one thing. I put the rest away, slide the case back under the bed and take the paper with my photograph to the wall. There are small nails there and some stones that will do for a hammer.

To the wall I affix the *Ahnenpass,* what is left of the girl I thought I was.

At breakfast, a boy with a mop of thick black hair walks in like some cowboy from an American film. Every girl turns and whispers to her neighbor. He is coming toward me. *It's Carissimi!* I think, for the first time in years. I'm suddenly nervous and fiddle with the top button of my blouse.

He slings his legs one at a time over the bench across from me and grins. I quickly look down and find something to do with my fork. He stares at me for a good twenty seconds, until I look up at him under my brows. He is impossibly good-looking, tan, his sleeves rolled up past his elbows to reveal strong, sinewy arms. My face feels hot and I get a soft pain in the middle of my chest. *Vittoria, mio core!*

"Hello," he says with a wink. "This seat taken?"

Obviously, it's not.

"Michah Gottlieb," he says, holding out his hand. "What's your name?"

"Gerta Rausch." I blush and barely touch his fingers.

"Got anybody left here?" He tears right into a piece of bread and takes a gulp of coffee.

"Um, no, I only had my father. He's gone."

"I'm sorry," he says, out of habit rather than conviction. "My mother died here, they tell me. Rivkah Gottlieb. She was a scientist." He takes a bite of meat. "Bastards."

"Oh, Michah! *You're* Michah?" All of a sudden, I feel a strange connection to him, like family. "Were you a boxer?"

He breaks into a surprised smile. "How did you know that? Did you know my mother?"

"We shared a bunk. I—I was with her when she died." Suddenly the color and the smile vanish from Michah's face. He puts down his fork and wipes his mouth. I put my hands in my lap.

"I thought she was crazy," I say. "She said she knew you were alive, you and Chaim. How could anyone know that . . ."

"Chaim." He lowers his eyes and swirls his coffee cup. "Chaim died in Auschwitz. He blew up the crematorium with his *Sonderkommando* group."

"Yes, I was there," I say solemnly. "I'll never forget it. The bravest thing I've ever seen. He probably saved thousands of lives. I heard that some of the women working in the munitions factory smuggled the gunpowder to them in their dress hems and under their fingernails."

He nods. "You were in Auschwitz, then?"

"Mm-hmm, the Women's Orchestra."

"Ah. 'And the band played on.' A lot of mixed feelings about you girls, from what I hear."

That stings. "It's not like I had a choice."

"No. Who did?" He shrugs. "Girls shouldn't have to endure those things. You should be able to recline on divans and eat bonbons."

We both smirk at this absurdity. "Ha. If only," I say. "I try to think that I gave a little comfort."

"That's human, at least," says Michah. "What did you play?"

"Viola. But to tell you the truth, I'm not very good. My father was the violist. He taught me how to play. That's the only reason I'm alive. I'm really a singer—or at least, I was going to be."

"Ah," he responds, barely listening. We turn to our food, detached, as images we'd rather not face start to fill the silence.

"So, Michah," I finally manage, "how did you survive?"

He chews slowly, thoughtfully, choosing his story.

"We're human beings again, Gerta. Let's not talk about our particulars. Let's talk about why I'm here. I'm taking people home."

"Huh," I scoff, and look blankly out of the far window, thinking again of Maria. "Where's home?"

"Right. Exactly. It's not in Europe. That much is obvious."

"How can you say that?" I puzzle. "*All* of Europe? That seems a stretch."

"Look around you, honey. Are they letting you leave this camp?"

"Well, no. But they're not going to keep us here forever. They're just trying to get through all the paperwork, that's why it's taking so long."

"Where do you plan to go?" he asks.

"I don't know. Somewhere with a conservatory. If not in Germany, then Paris, Milan—"

"You're just telling yourself that," he says. "There's no place for Jews in Europe anymore."

"I can't believe that."

"You haven't been outside the camps. Believe me. Europe is a hollow shell full of hollow men. Let me ask you, what do you know about Eretz Yisrael?"

I roll my eyes. "Oh, of course. You're not one of those 'destiny' types, are you?" I say, trying to tell myself I'm not one of those, either.

"I'm from the Haganah. The underground. *Shh*." He winks.

"The underground?" I huff. "What's the point? The Nazis are gone. Why be so secretive? Why not go back to Köln and start again?"

"I did go back. Köln is a total ruin. And where exactly do you think the Nazis *went*? They're back home, sweetheart, getting their jobs back, still in charge, but without the brown shirts. Do you think that once you get out of here, your neighbors will suddenly be in their right minds just because the war is over? That you'll somehow emerge into a *sane* world?"

"I guess I never thought about it." A whole town, a whole country, of Maria Büchners.

"Well, you have to face it. There's a past here, but no future. In a Jewish homeland, we have both. It's the only place we *can* go. And if enough of us join together, we can protect each other. Our own army, our own schools, where we don't always have to convince our neighbors that we don't, in fact, poison wells or make matzo with the blood of gentile children. Where *this* can't *possibly* happen again. Haven't you ever thought about it?"

"I'm *German*," I whisper-shout. I'm growing angrier, and I don't even know why. "My family's been here for centuries. Why shouldn't I stay in Europe?"

"Because they'll always see us as foreigners."

"But now that the world knows what the Nazis did to us? Come on, Michah, we're not hidden in the shadows anymore. Slowly but surely, we'll rebuild our lives. And what will happen if all the Jews leave? Then what? Then we're just a distant unknown to them and, yes, then the whole thing could happen again. We *have* to go back."

"Oh, my pretty little friend," Michah says, smiling with his mouth but not his eyes. "Don't you know your own history?"

My throat starts to tighten. I sniff hard—a trick Maria taught me to stop the tears from falling—and look away, folding my arms.

"Oh. I see," he says. "Never learned about your own people in your sweet German school? All that time, while the nurse was analyzing the color of your eyes and the length of your nose?"

"I didn't go to school. I had the *Ahnenpass*. I didn't know. . . ."

Several people are already finished and getting up to leave. I begin collecting my dishes to follow them. Michah reaches out and grabs my wrist.

"Listen to me carefully. Every single century for the past two thousand years has had its own version of Jewish destruction. This isn't new. Sixty years ago, it was the Russians. Before that, it was Damascus, and Spain, and England, and France, where they burned nine hundred Jews alive because they thought we masterminded the Plague. We've been in those countries for generations, too, right? Don't you think they would have realized by *now* they were wrong about us? After *two thousand* years?"

I have no answer. This stranger's hand is still clenching my wrist. I wrench free of his grasp.

"You're fooling yourself," he says, sopping up sauce with his last piece of bread.

"You don't know me!" I stand up suddenly and hit my knee on the table leg. The room goes silent. "You know nothing about me. I'm not some Zionist. I'm—I'm barely anything at all. And I don't have to be. I don't have to do any of this!"

I throw my napkin into my bowl and run out.

Back in my barracks, I crawl, weeping, under the worn blanket and soak my thin pillow with tears. I need my papa. *He* was my only home. Reaching under the bed, I draw out the viola case and tuck it in next to me. Its black leather covering warms to my body, and I cry myself to sleep, right in the middle of the morning.

My father's viola.

It is a forest. It is a living tree. It is the heartwood of our family. My father's viola is over two hundred years old, even older than Germany. It is the color of well-done pastry, shining like apricot glaze. Its fingerboard is molasses and its neck is honey. It is butter and creamy tea, as warm as Papa's arms, freckled like Papa's arms, strong and foundational like Papa's arms.

My father's viola does not scream; it pleads, it woos. It is the distant forest voice calling its child home at twilight. It soothes fever and melts like a lozenge over the throat. It is a blanket that warms but never stifles.

The tuning pegs are carved of some butterscotch wood, caressed into smooth rounds. Its chin rest is made of the same—what your cheek would be if it could. The chin rest is Papa's shoulder, Papa's chest, the hollow of Papa's collarbone. The f-holes are spindles of his pipe smoke on Sunday evenings by the radio. Two hundred years fade into the dark stain on its edges, smoke-black, dark as a forest river, dark as the plexus from which its song comes.

The viola's song is in a language no one knows; it reads from the alto clef, not the treble. It stays out of notice, but its absence is felt before it is named. It is the wisdom of the orchestra: the old woman who says almost nothing, except the one thing needed.

The instrument is alive in my hands; it trembles like a child who is too frightened to name her terror as she proceeds deeper into forest darkness, carrying a lantern of warm oil. I lay this child in her bed of blue velvet and hide her away at night where no one can find her. In my hard bunk in the orchestra barracks, I always used to put the case under my ankles so my father's viola would sleep in peace.

The viola is as much a part of my father as his hands or his voice. I carry him with me; we sing together as we dig secret tunnels to freedom.

CHAPTER 21

Outside the main camp gate is a secluded place I've been escaping to. The British guards know me; they know I will come back. I turn on a little charm, and all is understood. In the afternoons, before orchestra practice, I bring a sweater and a small square of old canvas tarp, in case I want to sit on the ground. Just past an old, flooded shed, the ground turns spongy under my heels and sends up the bready smell of decomposing grasses. My one pair of shoes is not up for this; the autumn mud works the muscles in my thighs until I come to the dry meadow path.

I walk slowly here, in and out through patches of sunlight like empty mansion rooms, methodically listening to each footstep press the grass. About midway through, the limbs of a stand of birch tree hold up the forest's form like women's bones. This grove has a magnetic pull, beckoning toward a carpet of blue-green mosses where I long to lie on my back and sing into the leaves. But it is a place where bodies were stacked, and I don't want to make friends with trees that once hid the dead.

The day's last flock of gray birds congregates above the seedheads of spent wildflowers and launches across the yellow green into a slate-blue sky. The waving stems scatter papery white moths, who go down again to hide in the dark grasses. Along the shrub-lined trail, I begin to raise both arms and turn around, around, dancing down the meadow path to a cricket chorus. I find one of their notes and sing with them. Louder I raise my voice until my rusty throat begins to burn with the song and I can feel a new breath come in—deep, past my lungs into my belly.

Something rustles in the brush: it freezes in place as we become aware of each other. A deer? Bear? Adrenaline rushes along the current between me and the unseen creature, and we are alert without seeing one another.

"Hello," I say in a plain voice. "Who's there . . ."

A figure emerges.

Michah.

His eyes are narrowed and he is smiling at me with an idea. He has a rucksack and a jacket tossed across one shoulder, and he is chewing on something. The breeze catches his hair and plays with three rogue locks.

"Nice song," he says. My heart begins to beat faster.

"I was just . . . ," I begin, my jaw tightening with the memory of our argument. "Never mind. I can go."

"Nonsense," he says, climbing over the brush. "I was about to head back. Don't let me stop you."

I take a step farther down the path. He changes course and joins me.

"Seems we had a fraught parting last time," he says. "Remind me of your name?"

"Gerta." Annoyed, nervous—I'm not sure what I am.

"Right. I didn't mean to upset you."

"I'm not upset. I mean, I was, but I was just all over the place, that's all."

I wish he would leave.

I hope he stays.

"You told me you were in the Women's Orchestra, right? Viola?" I look at him and concede with a little smile. "See? I remembered. I saw you last night at the concert, in the new camp band, didn't I?"

"Oh, I'm surprised you noticed," I say, abruptly pivoting on my coldness toward him. "How did we sound?"

"Ha—who am I to judge?" says Michah. "Sounded great to me. Must be nice to play for pleasure again."

"Yes. It's nice, yes. We're going to give a concert every Thursday night. You should come again. If you're not busy." I smooth my hair, suddenly conscious of what a walk in the woods will do to wild a person.

"I'll do that," he says.

We walk on, slowly choosing each step, talking about what we remember of Köln, about Chaim and Rivkah.

"Before the war," he says, "all my aunts and uncles came over on Sunday mornings for my mother's strudel. The cousins—we used to get so full of sugar, she'd kick us out and make us run in the park along the Rhine."

"The Rhine! I haven't thought about it since I was little. I remember, I used to ride along the river on the front of my mother's bicycle." It makes me ache. I can't bring myself, even now, to face the finality of the word *gone*.

The light is fading, and the whole meadow is covered in purple shadow. The amplified sounds of the forest floor under our feet make me realize we haven't said a word in several minutes. We come to a fallen tree in the path.

He climbs up and offers me his hand. I take it without thinking. In one motion he pulls me up and grabs me around the waist. I drop my sweater.

"You know, you have this look about you," he says, "like you're missing something." His face is uncomfortably close to mine and I can feel a heartbeat. It might be his; it might be mine. "I'm going to take three guesses as to what it might be."

One—he kisses my temple.

Two—my jawbone.

Three—an explosion of softness on my lips, the taste of apples and a recent cigarette.

He pulls his lips away so slowly, I feel like I'm being emptied into the space between us.

"Was I right?" he says, still grasping me close. His eyes are bottomless. A scar bisects his eyebrow. I take my deepest breath in months.

"Three more guesses," I say.

CHAPTER 22

Twilight.

I'm not sure I'm walking in a straight line. Licking my lips, electricity running through my fingertips, I drop my sweater again.

"Guten Abend, Fräulein," I hear a cheerful voice say behind me.

Lev picks up my sweater.

"Hi," I say, a bit annoyed to have my intoxication interrupted.

"Did you read my letter on Monday?" he asks in rapid, clipped words. "Maybe you're wondering why I wrote it. I mean, we see each other every day. It's just that my thoughts are clearer on a page than hanging out there in the air."

"Yes, it was . . . nice."

"Nice, as in 'nice to get'? Or 'it had nice things in it'?"

"You know, both, I guess." I just want him to hand me my sweater so I can go back to my room and meditate on the velvety feeling on my face.

He presses on. "Have you heard anything from the Brits? You know, any family willing to sponsor you?"

"No, I, um—"

"Because I've been searching. So far, I haven't found any relatives still alive. But I wondered if you had."

"No, no one. It was really just me and my father, you know." I'd rather think about anything else than this right now.

He sighs. "It's crazy—I had such a big family. There's got to be *someone* left. I just have to keep looking. You should, too. You never know!"

"I'm pretty sure there's no one," I say, curling my toes in my shoes.

"Well, God willing, there's someone out there waiting for both of us."

"Maybe." I feel the spell from Michah's kisses lifting away, and my skin tries desperately to cling to it.

"That reminds me of this time my uncles—they were twins, and they used to play this joke on everyone—"

Just then, Michah walks by under the streetlamp on the other side of the square. He catches my eye and winks at me. He's going toward a green army tent near a group of pine trees, camouflaged among the tents of real DPs. I didn't realize that's where he stayed. But of course—he's not officially supposed to be here. This is how he must live, going from camp to camp, blending in and recruiting people to go to Palestine.

He's going to leave, I think. *I can't let him leave.*

Lev is still talking.

"Lev," I interrupt, "I've got to go. I'm sorry." I jog toward the tent.

"All right. But, Gerta!" he calls after me. "Will you meet me tomorrow?

In the grove, before supper. I left another letter for you. I have something to ask you—I wrote it in there."

"Sure," I call back indifferently. "See you tomorrow."

"Wait!" he calls. "Your sweater!" I run back to take it, but Lev holds on for an extra moment. "Tomorrow," he says softly. "Tomorrow, then."

CHAPTER 23

"Gerta."

"Hello, Lev." I can't look at him; I squint at the cold light on the distant field.

"Thanks for meeting me here," he says.

I look at his shoes. I never realized how meticulously he keeps them polished. "We meet here every day, Lev."

"You know what I mean." Like a little boy, he picks up a dried seedhead and plays with it, not looking at me, either.

"Right. Your letter. I read it."

"All right. So . . . let's talk."

But we don't talk. We just stay there fidgeting until the meal announcement. I don't know what to do with his letter, and he doesn't know how to just *say it*.

The bell rings for supper.

"Should we—" he fumbles.

"Yes, let's talk inside. It's freezing out here."

We walk into the dining hall in silence. There is the warm, yeasty smell of fresh bread and roasted chicken. Trays of bright red fruit pudding wait at the end of the line. But it feels like a feast for someone else.

Suddenly Lev thrusts his hand back and grabs mine. I know this isn't done where he comes from. But he is holding my hand. His fingertips are stained with ink. His palm is rough. I can feel his pleading in the squeezing of my fingers. And just as quickly, he lets go; he seems stunned at himself for acting on such an impulse.

He takes his plate from the server and we find a seat. Someone has put

jars of dried branches on the tables, arranged with stems of seedheads from the field where I kissed Michah. Lev sits down across from me.

"Gerta."

A leaf falls from a branch, and I press my fingernail into the space between its veins, cracking it into pieces.

"Gerta, do you know what I'm asking you?"

"Yes, Lev. I wish you hadn't." Nervously, I rub the tiny fragments of dried leaf into dust between my fingers.

He leans in close, suddenly earnest. He crosses his arms to avoid repeating his lapse in judgment. His pale lashes reveal the world behind his hazel eyes, and that world is trembling, dangling, like a lone bright planet in dark space.

"Let me put it this way, Gerta. Do you see these people around us? Each one of them is in the same situation as you and me: trying to find a way not to be alone. I'm not talking about being in love, exactly, if that's not what you want. Maybe we've both been through too much for that. We could just be . . . friends. For life."

"But we're *babies*, Lev."

He looks down at his hands. "In Kielce, I would have had a wife and a child by now."

"I'm not from Kielce."

"No. And I'm not from Köln."

I stare at the fragments of leaves under my fingers. I don't dare tell him about Michah.

"I don't know how you feel about me, Gerta. But somehow, I think, when the chance for love—or something like it—comes up alongside you, you should take a walk with it. See it as a gift, or at least an opportunity."

"Okay, Lev," I say at last. "There was a boy in my choir, Rudolf. We liked each other. A lot. He asked his parents if he could study viola with my father just so he could come to my house. He'd stand there staring stupidly at me the whole time. But just like that, he stopped coming, with no explanation. Maybe he moved on to another girl. Boys are fickle. It's like my father used to say: 'The only constant in this world is change.'"

"I don't see things that way," Lev says sincerely.

"Maybe not, but what makes you different from him? You and I are friends, yes, but once we're out of here, who's to say one of us won't change our mind?"

"I have no intention of changing my mind."

"Lev," I say, "we're friends. But you want a *wife*, not a 'friend for life.' I want to get out of here and live before I even think about *marriage*. Besides, until all this happened, I didn't even know I was Jewish. And my experience of what that means? It's *this* place. It's fear. It's death. I don't want that life. I don't know a god, I don't know a family, I don't even know myself. I might be a horrible person after all."

"I don't have any answers, either, Gerta. I want to rediscover what it means to be Jewish for myself, too. I want to learn again who I am, who we are. Who is going to teach it to us? We have to figure it out either way. Couldn't we help each other do that, together?"

I push the food around on my plate. This is a veritable banquet placed before me. Just a short time ago, I would have given anything for one forkful of this meal.

"No," I say, rising. I leave my plate on the table. "No, I'm not the one you want."

IV

DISPLACED

Bergen-Belsen

Spring–Summer 1946

CHAPTER 24

Spring is finally burgeoning after the longest winter, and the birches' new leaves turn their faces toward the sun's warmth. Just around this time last year, I was starving to death here in Bergen-Belsen, doubting whether I would even live. The new greens and pinks on the trees are magnificent. Color seeps deeper into me now, and I can hear more distinct sounds. Bread no longer tastes like death. The scent of rotten corpses is gone from the air at last. The breeze whispers a hint of cool, perfumed blossom, and I have a red sweater, a yellow overcoat.

I'm beginning to thaw.

But I still can't sing. I'm coming to realize that my voice must be gone for good.

Nights are hardest. It takes me hours to fall asleep. I focus on every muscle and bone, every reality of my own body, trying to get back into *now*. First I press my fingertips together as hard as I can and let the sensation run up my arm, to my shoulder, my neck, across my collarbone to the other side. I go all the way down, until I'm pointing and flexing each toe, one by one.

I can fill out my brassiere now, can't count my ribs quite so easily. I run a hand over my stomach and recall Michah's arms wrapping around my waist from behind, surprising me on my walk to practice, exploring my neck with soft kisses.

I've never had thoughts like this. It's different from counting crumbs of bread with that wild, hollow look in the eyes, just trying to stay alive. The fantasies that run through my mind aren't like the childish ones I had before the camps: dreams of wandering through cool, dark forests, catching fairies hidden among ferns. Now there's someone hiding behind those trees, a boy with a dark, heavy brow and glittering eyes, always laughing, living loud and bright and magnetic, always there with the tang of smoke on his lips.

Days, I spend most of the time in school, in rehearsal with the musical society, or in the crowd surrounding Michah and his maps. But sometimes I walk by the grove and watch Lev pace with his prayer book. He looks transcendent as he rhythmically bows, murmuring the Hebrew prayers that he learned on his father's knee.

Two men in woolen flat caps are sitting on a makeshift bench near the camp gate, talking over the headlines in *Unzer Sztyme*. Reports have started to calculate how many Jews have died since the exterminations began.

"Some are saying five, six million."

"Impossible. Were there even six million Jews in the world?"

"They are saying it's two out of every three of us across Europe—gone. Vanished." He makes a gesture like smoke dispersing into the air.

At first I am as incredulous as the other man. How did *any* of us survive? Did anyone manage to stay hidden until the end? Papa tried to make us two of the invisible ones; Lev wore his identity on his sleeve. Neither of us knew anything different. What religion was to his family, music was to mine—but ultimately, we both got swept into the net. How is it that people very far away had calculated, in an arithmetic known only to them, *what* and *who* we were?

Tonight, as I come in, the girls in my room are setting each other's hair with bits of rag and smoking cigarettes with the windows open.

"There's something there for you, Gerta," says Roza.

Wedged between my pillow and the metal bed frame is a letter. It's been three months since Lev and I have spoken. I know his schedule and try to avoid seeing him. When we do see each other, there's a quick smile, and I go numb. My chest gets tight and I just want to run. That letter. Those questions.

This one is different.

Dear Gerta,

   Even with this distance between us, you're still my closest friend.

   I've been writing my memories down, the good ones . . . and the horrors, too. It helps—I sleep a little better. Not so many nightmares.

   But I miss sharing it all with you. If we can't talk, I'd like to write to you, unless you tell me to stop.

   Look for my stories soon.

                                        Lev

I can't deny that I miss Lev, our talks in the grove. His stories—he's told me pieces, mostly the good parts, as I've told him. Our favorite foods.

Games we played as children. Songs our mothers and fathers sang. Pranks we played; the ways friends could be cruel. Things we would never have told our fathers.

"Which boyfriend is it from, Gerta?" asks Roza, with something of the *old* Roza in her tone.

I put the letter in the shoebox under my bed. "Mind your own business," I say, and curl up to look at my photographs.

The stories of the living are all of one piece: a million colors along the same thread.

CHAPTER 25

The air is heavy with an impending storm, and my head is throbbing. I can't concentrate on my viola études. If Papa were here, he'd be snapping his fingers in my face to wake me up. The hall is empty and darkening. Suddenly I have an impulse to get up, stand at the edge of the stage and open my mouth to sing.

Just one note. I try to occupy the hall with my voice, but I can't fill my belly with enough breath. My vocal cords feel like dried, crackled rubber bands. When I try to push my diaphragm down, my middle hurts and my legs begin to tremble. And then, something else.

It begins with a very slight, warm sensation, something I haven't felt in three years. It feels like I've wet myself, but no—this is not a stream but a pool. I know what this is. I grab my sweater and tie the sleeves tight around my waist. I can't risk running, but I walk as fast as I can to the latrines. There are many women there, and they give me knowing looks. And there, also, is Roza.

"You too, hmm?" she says. She gestures toward the sweater around my waist while I shiver in the drizzling rain. She chews her nails as she waits for a stall. "I don't know whether to be happy or sad about it."

"Me neither, if it's what I think it is," I say.

"They must have . . . you know, things for us in the medical building," she offers. "I can wait for you if you want to go together."

"Okay." My neck is starting to sweat. I just want to get into the stall and not talk about this anymore.

"I was kind of resigned to it," Roza says. "Never having babies, I mean. I guess this is a sign of hope, right?"

"Right," I say vacuously, tightening the knotted sleeves.

Thankfully, I catch it early enough that I don't completely ruin my clothes. My belly is cramping hard, and I'm aware of long-dormant places within myself.

Roza's waiting for me, and we head to see the nurse.

"You all right?" she asks.

"What?" I dismiss the question. "I'm fine."

"No, you're not. I can tell. I mean, you're always quiet, Gerta, but not *this* quiet. And you've always got this look." She stops and shows me: furrowed brow, down-turned mouth, shoulders hunched to the ears.

"Do I really?" I had no idea it was so obvious; I straighten up. "Sorry. I, uh, tried singing today."

"Oh. Not good, I take it?"

"It's gone. Just gone. Something must have happened from the typhus. Scarring, infection, I don't know. But my voice isn't coming back."

She sidles up and nudges me sympathetically. "Don't say that."

"It's true. I have nothing. I have this viola, and I can't even play it right. I'm terrible."

"You're not terrible! You live and breathe music, Gerta. You're going to be okay. You'll at least be able to find work."

She doesn't understand. The past and the future are clouding together, and I don't know what's real.

"Maybe, in some small-town orchestra somewhere. But I'm realizing that my life isn't going to be anything like I thought. *Nothing* like I thought."

CHAPTER 26

The morning is dark and I'm in bed too long. Outside, the rain pats the muddy walkways between the buildings. The other girls in my room don't seem to want to go out, either. The room is warm, the air is clean, and my mind is clear. From under the blanket, I'm watching the drops catch each other on the windowpane. There's a knock at the door.

At the other end of the long room, one of the girls answers it, and a figure stands in the doorway. His silhouette shows a full beard and curly sidelocks. He has a letter, but he does not hand it to her directly, instead putting it down on a table by the door and saying something to her, as hushed as the rain. He leaves, and she comes to my bed and hands the letter to me.

There are thousands of people in this camp. Many of them have gone back to their religion. There are rabbis—why doesn't Lev talk to *them*? He's probably seen me with Michah. I don't know what he expects from me now.

And yet there's this letter—and the daylight seems to have gotten a little brighter.

Dear Gerta,

Nothing I write must surprise you. We've been through similar things, but I want you to understand where I've come from.

I don't know if you'll even read this. Maybe you'll just throw it away. But if you do read it, maybe you'll know me a little better.

I had just turned thirteen and become bar mitzvah when I started my apprenticeship at the Yiddish newspaper in Kielce. Ever since I was little, my father and I had read the newspaper every morning, and we both knew that was the trade for me. Whenever he would take me with him to the print shop, the smell of the ink, sharp and sweet, made me dizzy, and I was addicted to it. The giant rolls of newsprint, the rhythmic clacketing of the press—I loved it all. It was work I could feel. *Do you know what I mean?*

You said you thought I was a scholar. Well, I didn't do that well at yeshiva, but copying the passages down in class felt kind of holy, the same kind of magic as the letters appearing on the press. And I had some ideas about getting the newspaper out beyond our community to others in Poland someday. I grew up hearing my father's friends talk about religious divisions in the town, but I thought there must be more that unifies us than divides us. Maybe if we had a newspaper for the whole region, people could exchange their ideas and have a chance to make up their own minds.

I was only a year into my apprenticeship when the ghetto was formed. My mother and sisters were at the height of Passover preparations. Dishes and linens were everywhere. They gave our whole town an hour to pack as much as we could carry. Then they crammed us all in together. My family of ten was shoved into half of our house, and another family, which had about a thousand little children, moved into the other half. We felt like canned fishes, and it was awkward to sleep and dress in a room with my sisters. We had to take shifts, waiting outside the door, to let them have privacy. The other family's daughters lived in my father's library, where I had always escaped when my siblings got on my nerves. There was no place to be alone now, no place to collect my thoughts or immerse myself in words.

It wasn't long before food became scarce. Hunger caused a lot of fighting—people weren't thinking straight. Jews were shot in the street every day for no reason, and I was scared to even raise my eyes to look at the SS. I still worked at the print shop, but we didn't get to print what we wanted. I'm sure you can imagine.

My parents tried to keep the family's spirits up, my mother forcing herself to sing as she struggled to make food out of air, and my father and I still secretly studied the forbidden Torah and prayed in whispers. My brothers became very creative in the black market. It was amazing what a bit of scarce butter could do to bring a family together.

That's all for now. I'll write again,

Lev

I slowly put the letter down and picture Lev's life before I met him, going backward in time.

I think of him running down the street, a little red-haired boy in a sweater-vest. Sitting in class. Playing keep-away with his sister. Wrestling with his brother. Falling asleep in the arms of his mother.

People of *Lev's*, people I will never know.

It's all so completely . . . unfair.

The rain has stopped. I need to get out of here.

CHAPTER 27

"Michah!" I call, running across the puddle-specked courtyard. He is standing at a table covered with maps, talking to other men but surrounded by girls, prettier ones than me. Their clothes are hand-me-downs, too, but somehow smarter than mine. They've got too much makeup on and their hair is up in curls and twists, and I can see the lean, hungry look in their eyes, for Michah. They all jostle each other for a closer position. But they don't know what I know: the spicy scent of his skin, the feeling of his slight whiskers on my cheek, the rhythm of his warm breath in my ear—and I need that now, to feel like I'm inside my own body.

"Michah!" I call again, this time looking at the girls as I say it, smiling and narrowing my eyes at them. They have nothing on me. He finally looks up and catches my stare. He tells the men to wait and elbows past the girls as he comes toward me.

"Hello, *you*," he says, putting his arm around my waist. He ushers me to a dark passageway out of sight. The afternoon sun doesn't reach us, and it's chilly back here. He pushes me against the brick wall of the bunk hall and begins kissing my neck. It is delicious, and I drink it in like nectar. His kisses are masterful and require nothing of me. His arms surround me and I let myself, for this moment, forget where I am.

"Come with us, honey," he says, between nibbles on my ear. "It's almost time. We're leaving for Eretz Yisrael soon."

How easy he makes it sound. "All right, when do we leave?"

"That's the spirit," he whispers. "Just a couple more months. I've got the route mapped out and a guy making up papers for everyone."

A thought tugs me back. "Wait—" I stop and put a hand on his chest. "I have a friend . . . he might want to come, too."

"No stowaways, little girl. I handpick my passengers." Suddenly his breath is too hot on my neck. I look at his eyes. He is somewhere else, not with me. He is trying to kiss me again, but he looks like a bird trying to peck for a crust of bread.

"I have to go," I say, slipping out from between him and the wall.

"Come see me again, honey," he calls. Out of the corner of my eye, I see him straighten his jacket and run his fingers through his hair.

I'm not sure where I'm walking—just away.

When you're angry and you've just had a kiss that you somehow wish you hadn't, you might not look where you're walking as carefully as you should. I smash into him.

Not Michah.

Lev.

"Gerta! I'm so sorry. Are you all right?" He's holding my arms to steady me. Not two minutes ago, I was this close to Michah. I'm dizzy and I just want to run.

"Sorry, I was . . . just leaving. Sorry, Lev."

He takes a step back and straightens his kippah. "Wait, Gerta—I've been leaving some letters for you. Have you . . . gotten a chance to read them?"

I stop short. His eyes are wide, searching, depending on me to say yes.

"Lev," I say, "I've read them all. Over and over."

"Oh, good," he sighs. "They weren't too . . . intense?"

I chuckle. "Too intense? What could possibly be too intense?"

"Well, the way I . . . never mind. It's not like you don't know these things for yourself."

I fall inward: a sad smile, a subtle, resigned shrug. "I only know my own story. Not yours."

"True," he acknowledges, clasping his hands behind his back.

"Please write more, Lev."

"Really?" His question is quiet, guarded. "You want me to?"

"There's something about the way you write. It's . . . how do I describe it . . . It's important."

Wordless, we instinctively walk toward our grove.

"Lev, I have to tell you, I'm sorry we—"

"There's something I left out of the last letter," he interrupts. "About my life before." He draws a long breath. "I was engaged."

"*What?*" I ask, too loudly. "Lev, how is that possible? What were you, twelve?"

"Fifteen. In my town, they found you a trade, they found you a wife, you studied. It's just what you *did*. Her name was Shayna."

The name of this unknown girl makes me hold my breath. Questions want to tumble out of me. *Was she pretty? Why do I care?*

"Were you really going to get *married*?"

"I know, I know, we were just children. But no one knew if they had to-morrow. It just made everyone feel like they had to move faster."

"What was she like?" I ask, trying to sound nonchalant.

"Well, I'm not sure, really. I didn't really *know* her. Do you remember the family with the thousand children I wrote about living in my house? She was the oldest. I started to like her. Of course, we didn't come close, just spoke across the table. But everyone could tell we were looking at each other in *that way*. I was already starting to see her as my future."

"She must have been hard to resist." My cheeks start to warm.

"She was beautiful. Consumed my imagination . . ." He trails off. "We managed to stay together on the transport. Once we were on the train, we were pressed together, a hundred people to a car."

"I know how that was."

"She was crushed against me completely. So I held her. What else could I do? She struggled to breathe; I could feel her chest heaving against mine. In any other situation, I would have enjoyed it. At first, I admit, I did. It was

comforting, even a little thrilling. But it became . . . unbearable. For all those countless hours, I couldn't escape her. I wanted her to go away. I couldn't wait to peel myself from her, but she just clung to me. I remember, she gripped my shirt so tightly, her knuckles were white.

"When she had to relieve herself, even then she wouldn't leave me, so we rolled together to the bucket, kind of like a sheet through a mangler, you know? I couldn't even turn away, so I at least gave her the dignity of closing my eyes.

"The bucket became useless after a while, with a hundred people's slop in it, and eventually there was nothing to do but go right where you stood. The heat, the stench—it was overwhelming. I just threw my head back to gasp at any amount of air. I couldn't think of anything but how to detach myself from Shayna."

His mouth sticks; his words are punctuated with short, shallow breaths. I turn to face him. I don't want him to have to say this into the air. I want him to tell it to *me*.

"We finally stopped, and they pried open the doors. We practically fell out. I was grateful to take a deep breath, even though the air was just rotten with that . . . that smoke. But not everyone got off the train. Several children had suffocated. At least five, six old people had had heart attacks. Once the pressure was relieved, their corpses crumpled to the floor. They were dragged out and thrown in the mud like rag dolls. A woman went over to the body of her little boy, and they hit her in the head with the butt of a gun.

"I'm not sure if I was imagining it or not, but I remember music. I wonder if it was your orchestra, or the men's. It was a march, like at a town parade. My head was swimming. There was so much confusion and shouting, and the music made it seem like a bizarre circus. Right away, they started separating us: men to the right, women and children to the left. Shayna gripped my hand. Her eyes were panicked. They herded us into the lines, and she pawed at my arms. Her line was marched away toward that plume of smoke in the distance, and she was crying for me . . . she was saying, 'Lev . . . help me . . . don't leave me. . . .' "

He is mouthing the words more than saying them. Tears stand in his eyes but don't fall.

"I felt the hot wind go through my clothes, like hell. There were gray ashes everywhere, sticking to my sweat."

You can never get clean enough from that, I want to say.

"It didn't take long to realize what had happened to Shayna, my parents, my siblings. I held on to the memory of her body the whole time, as if she were slipped inside my own clothes, always with me. That was the last time I saw any girl or any woman alive—until they laid you next to me. Beautiful Gerta, with a song in your eyes, even through that fever . . ."

For some reason, it doesn't bother me that he said that.

He finally looks at me squarely. "I'm not supposed to touch a girl I'm not related to, you know."

"I guessed that," I say. "But you've fed me soup, wiped my sweaty forehead. Lev, you caught me when I fainted. . . ."

"That's different. Those were emergencies."

"But you—you grabbed my hand."

"I know." His face is full of pain. "That was a mistake, Gerta. I'm sorry. It all made sense in my mind—I just assumed you would say yes and that it would be all right. Now I feel . . . like I stole something from you."

"You didn't steal from me, Lev. You were caring."

That doesn't assuage his uneasiness. "But caring doesn't feel like that to me," he counters. "I don't want to take anything, from anyone. Caring feels like letting *you* decide who to let in. And you've made it clear that it isn't me."

"It's not that, it's just—"

"I'm only telling you this because you let me, and you listen. But if you want me to stop writing, or if you want me to stay away—"

"No, it's okay. I don't want you to go. We can keep it this way—letters, talking. Just . . . no pressure. No *should*s," I say.

"No *should*s," he agrees.

CHAPTER 28

"Guess what?" says Roza as we're walking to school. "I've gotten back almost all the Schumann songs! Even 'Hasche-Mann,'—you know, the one with all those crazy runs? I can't play it staccato yet, but I've got the notes down. Slow as syrup, but *correct*!"

"Roza, that's fantastic!" I give her a quick side-hug. "Are you going to give a recital?"

"Maybe in a couple of months, sure! I need more practice, though."

"You're obsessed. All you do is practice. It's really working, too. You're getting very good."

She slows her pace. "I was always good."

"Well . . ." I'm not sure if I should tell her the truth.

"What?"

"I mean, you played notes, but that doesn't mean you were *good*. It was just a little . . . mechanical. But wait, I don't mean it like that," I add quickly, trying to undo my blunder. "You're fine now! You're *getting* there."

She stops completely. "I didn't know that's how you felt, Gerta. We play together every *day*. Have you just been humoring me?"

"N-no, of course not," I stammer. "I was just trying to be encour—"

"If you want to talk about 'playing notes,'" Roza hisses, "*you* don't really play viola. You just do it because you're scared to sing."

"That's different," I protest. "I *can't* sing."

"I don't believe that for a moment. If you truly wanted it like you always said you did, you'd find a way to do it. I did."

"Right," I say, remembering her gloating with the girls in Theresienstadt. "Because you're perfect."

"What's that supposed to mean?"

"Even though we've been through the same exact nightmare, you find a way to hold that over me. Like you even *survive* better than me. You always have to be on top."

"That is ridiculous. Gerta, where is this coming from?"

"Hmmph. Saint Roza the Overcomer." I wave a benediction in the air.

"You're being a brat," she says with disgust. "Play viola if you want. Don't sing, then. I don't care."

"I'm fine as is. You're jealous because I have something you don't."

She's incredulous and puts her hands on her hips. "What do *you* have that I don't?"

"Michah." His name feels like triumph.

"You can't be serious. You don't *have* him. He never even says your name."

"That's a horrible thing to say."

"But you know I'm right. You've got this other boy—what's his name, Lev?—following you around like a happy puppy; meanwhile, *Meee-chah* sneezes and you run half a mile across the camp to bring him a tissue. He's got other girls, you know."

"He's not perfect," I say defensively. "We have an arrangement."

"Do you?" she challenges.

At least in my mind, we do. "Mind your own business, Roza. I don't even know why we're fighting. Let's stick to music."

"Is this about Lev? Did he ask you again?"

"No. Absolutely not. I don't want Lev."

"Huh," she huffs. "You don't know *what* you want."

I slow down, kicking up a cloud of dust. Before I know what I'm saying, my heart speaks. "I want the orange trees."

"The what?"

"They used to keep them in a greenhouse over the winter, but one day in spring they'd wheel out all the enormous pots and line the paths of the Residenz gardens with them. You'd smell perfume in the air for days until the petals fell off, like snow in spring. I used to pick up piles of them and rain them down over my papa's head. But we weren't allowed to pick the fruit. I would have given anything to taste one of those oranges."

"You want the orange trees."

"I want to taste the fruit."

"Gerta," Roza says at the school door, "the viola isn't the fruit. Singing is."

The clarity of this stuns me.

"I never thought I was better than you, by the way," she confesses. "I was scared of you. Because you were the real thing."

I sit down at my desk and stare at my hands, ashamed of judging her, of holding on to petty competitions that no longer exist.

Finally, I pull a crumpled letter from my skirt pocket. This must be the fifth time I've read this one.

Gerta,

You've helped me discover something: I never would have guessed how much I love writing. When we were in the ghetto, my mentor used to tell us in the shop, "Yidden, schreibt un farschreibt"—"Jews, write it all down." Words, Gerta, they're proof of life. Having something written, or printed, means that what you thought was happening really did happen. That when the Nazis came with their new definitions, you could point to what was written down and say, "No, this is the truth. I'm not crazy."

Maybe you're the only person who will ever read my story. That's enough for me. At least you and I will know the truth together.

After that first selection at Auschwitz, I was miraculously reconnected with my mentor. They put him in charge of a floor in the munitions factory because he was so precise. When he saw me, he took an enormous risk: he pointed at me and shouted, "That boy—he is my apprentice! I need him! He is the most skilled and talented machinist I have ever employed." He was lying, of course. But I had to learn quickly. Both of our lives depended upon his words becoming true.

I was in Auschwitz for two years. I only survived because I was on a good assignment, like you—not hard labor hauling stones or digging ditches in the snow. But toward the end, they needed a machinist to keep the elevators from the gas chambers to the ovens running smoothly. When the "processing" was getting too slow, they made me help put the bodies in. I thought I would lose my mind.

Then my mentor was finally selected. Gassed. He was like a father to me, Gerta, the last person I knew from Kielce. He kept me alive, moving me forward, teaching me more than I ever needed to know.

I was on duty the day he was murdered. I saw him on the pile and put his body in the oven myself. Usually they put them in three at a time to burn faster, but I rushed him in by himself to make sure he had the dignity of his own cremation. And is that "dignity"? Is that what that word came to mean?

It was the best I could do for him.

We do the best we can for each other, don't we?

Lev

That night, I go to Roza and sit on the edge of her bed in the moonlight.

I gently pick up her gnarled hand and put her fingers up to her face. "Do you see these?" Then I bring her fingers to touch my throat. "Do you feel this? This is what it cost us to survive. We all paid with some part of ourselves. None of us escaped unbroken."

"Of course not." She shakes her head. This is something she's already discovered.

"And Lev doesn't 'follow me around.' He fights for what he cares about—in ways even you and I can't understand. He's my friend. I've earned the right to be friends with whomever I want. Even with *you*." I chuckle.

"Oh, thanks." She laughs back.

"It's amazing when you think about it, isn't it? Even through all we've lost, somehow we keep living. You *choose* to keep playing with your twisted fingers. I choose to keep playing my papa's viola. Lev—he chooses to keep praying. We just all have to do it broken."

CHAPTER 29

A couple of weeks go by. I've had a great rehearsal, a beautiful Beethoven string quartet. The workday is over, and Lev is washing ink off his hands. I decide to wait for him outside the print shop. He comes out smiling, straightening his new wide-brimmed black hat.

"Do you like it?"

I laugh. "You look like an old man."

"What do you mean? This is a good hat. My father had one just like it."

"Exactly," I say, smirking. "But it's very distinguished, Lev, really." It's hard to suppress my smile. It feels good to walk with him, even if he does look like a grandfather.

"It reminds me of who I am," he says. "Who I used to be—maybe who I can still be." The spring breeze blows on our faces, gentle and warm.

"Thanks for your letters," I say. "You know, all through the winter, I was worried you wouldn't want to talk to me anymore, after I asked you—after what happened. I was sure you were mad at me."

"Impossible. I could never be mad at you."

"Oh, yes, you could." I laugh, swinging the viola case. "Give it time."

"Why, because of that boy you're with?"

A sting hits my chest and I'm . . . ashamed. "I wondered if you knew about that."

"I do," he says plainly. "You always said that's what you wanted, didn't you? A carefree lover."

"Is that what I said?" I cringe. "It sounds terrible when you say it."

"You're my friend. I want you to be happy. Who am I to judge? You and I, we're just not meant to be."

When I hear him say that, it feels wrong. Lev, of all people, deserves to be happy—it just can't be with *me*.

"Are you?" he asks. "Happy, I mean."

We're walking so slowly; Lev walks heel to toe with great deliberateness. My legs feel suddenly heavy as sandbags, and minuscule particles float in front of my eyes.

"I think we both know the answer to that," I say. "Are *you* happy?"

"No," he admits. "But—I think I could be. Someday."

My heart sinks a little.

"It couldn't have worked out anyway, Lev."

"I know, you're right. I picture a certain life—an observant wife, a Jewish home. Quiet, simple. Printing papers by day, coming home to a family at night. My dream hasn't changed."

"You should have it, Lev," I say, looking at him solemnly. "Every part."

"As you should have your dream, Gerta."

"My dream . . ."

"Your music. I watch your face when you play. There's something there. It's not happiness, exactly. It's . . . joy. Pain too. But joy."

"I'll have to think about that." I squint at the late sun. "I never thought about joy."

"It's like watching you live a lifetime in each piece you play."

He's right about that. "A hundred lifetimes, really."

"Your whole being sings. That's how I feel about Torah."

"I know. I watch you praying sometimes." He stops. I can't tell if he's embarrassed or not.

"You have your father's instrument," he says. "I have my father's faith. It's the best part of us. We survived with the best part of us still intact."

I'm still not sure about that. The best part of me feels torn and sloppily stitched back together. We're standing here with our hearts too open, and I have to do something with this cavernous sensation.

"Come here, Lev. I want to show you something." I lead him to a bench and open my viola case. "Hold this." I hand him the viola and start rosining the bow.

"What am I going to do with this?" He laughs.

"You're going to play it. Hold it with your left hand, and rest it on your shoulder, like that. Nice and soft, under your chin. Right. Now hold the bow, like this. Put your pinkie on top so it doesn't flop around."

An awkward grin spreads across Lev's face. The viola shakes in his hand.

"Here, you don't have to hold the neck. Don't worry, I'll make the notes. You just move the bow back and forth. When I touch the tip of the bow, tilt it up or down, and that will make you play the different strings." I stand a little to the back of Lev's shoulder and hold the fingerboard. "This is a piece I used to play with my papa. It's Schumann's 'Träumerei.' It means 'Daydream.' You'll like it."

We play the slow melody together. I'm surprised that the bow doesn't squeak on the strings as Lev pulls it.

"You have a sensitive touch, Lev. Good rhythm." I play in time with Lev's breath, breathing in the warm trace of printer's ink on his skin. The nervous laughter is gone, but his lips quiver.

We finish the last note; I take the viola from his shoulder, and we just look at each other.

"Beautiful," he says. "I could do that forever. The way it kind of . . . hums through your heart . . ."

"I know. I know."

"Gerta." I see how he's looking at me, and I have to change the subject. I just blurt out the first thing that comes to mind.

"I had this dream almost every night in Auschwitz that I had a whole barrel of water to myself. It was this huge, golden vessel, and I had a silver cup, and I'd just dip the cup in and pour the water all over my head, in my mouth, spilling it over my face and clothes. Then the water would rise and soak me up to the knees. And it was crazy, because it was always icy cold and refreshing when I drank it, but warm and soothing like a bath when I was standing in it. Isn't that strange?"

He starts laughing.

"What's so funny?"

"I—I don't know—" He has this rapid, musical laugh, like a little boy's, and I see him like that, a little boy with a big hat, and it's as if we're in the wrong bodies, in the wrong lives. His laugh is so contagious that I can't help laughing, too. We're losing our composure, doubling over, our bellies and faces aching.

"Warm and cold. Young and old," he says, still laughing, wiping hilarious tears from his eyes.

I'm trying to catch my breath, and I realize I don't even get the joke.

"Lev, what are you *talking* about?"

"It's just—we're so young, but we're ancient, you know? We've grown as old as it's possible to *get*. Oh, Gerta," he sighs and laughs at the same time, "I wanted to grow *young* with you."

All of a sudden, I'm looking into Lev's eyes. They see me, and somehow they *know* me. They are unwriting my careful script. They're the eyes that broke my fever. I can't escape this . . . this *knowingness* of his.

I look seriously at him now as the laughter slows. "But I can't come with you, where you're going."

"Where am I going?" he asks, with this mixture of confusion and hope.

"To your faith. To God." I start slowly wiping down the viola with a soft cloth. "I can't go there."

He traces the scrolled top of the instrument with his finger. "You don't think so, but with your music—you're closer than you think."

"I mean, I guess, but—what has He done for you, for all your faith? He took away everything, everyone we loved. . . ."

"I'm not sure *who* took them, Gerta," he says, suddenly sober. "Who? Hitler? The SS?"

"Obviously," I answer, somewhat perplexed. I nestle the viola and bow back in the case. "I mean, maybe. But He *let* it—"

"Or was it our neighbors? The ones who wanted your house, or your silver, because to them you were already as good as dead? The boys in town who made fun of you for being different? Or was it the *Kapo* who shut the gas chamber doors? The guard who dumped in the Zyklon B pellets? The *Sonderkommando* who threw our parents' bodies into the ovens? *Who*, Gerta? Who killed them? You think it was *God*? A lot of people got in line to butcher us before 'God' had anything to do with it!" His voice breaks. He is getting hysterical. "I don't know who. I don't know. I don't—"

My eyes are fixed, dry and hot, on the swirling orange clouds ahead of us.

"It's okay, Lev. It's all right. I'm sorry. I shouldn't have said anything."

But he is beginning to sob and punch his thigh and cough, and he can't stand up straight. He's still thinner than he should be: the hollow of his stomach, the caved-in cheeks. Before I know what is happening, my arms come up under his, and he falls into me, heaving hard into my neck, washing my skin with answerless tears.

"I'm sorry, Lev. I'm sorry." I hold him, but then he is gripping me around my shoulders and clenching the back of my blouse, my hair. "I'm here, Lev. Right here."

And he just can't let go of me. Right now, I am his mother, his sister, his Shayna, and he can't let go. So I hum "Träumerei" again and I sway him, rocking, a lullaby, a prayer. He lets me, and I feel that vibration in my stomach—that presence.

I feel like I could do this, falling into each other, forever. With Lev.

Singing to him, holding each other's sorrow. He begins to calm, with just the barest catch in his breath, and he releases my blouse, my shoulders.

Lev looks at me close, his eyelids puffy and red, his pale lashes disappearing around hazel pools. He lifts his hand and touches my eyebrow. He traces the bone beneath my eye, my cheek, my upper lip, trembling like he did holding the viola.

It's then that he remembers himself and retreats, a look of terror in his eyes, as though waking from a trance, his eyes shifting back and forth as he stares at me in fear.

"I have to go," he says. Lev pulls down on his vest and wipes his eyes. He smooths his clothes and his short beard and backs away.

"Goodbye, Gerta."

CHAPTER 30

Slowly, at the camp high school, I'm learning about where I come from, the peculiar yesterdays of my people. I learn songs, foundations of religion, a prayer or two. As unfamiliar as Judaism still is, there's a feeling of homecoming about it all. I have hazy dreams of my mother every night.

Tonight there's been some lecture in the dining hall on medieval Jewish history, and it's gotten out late. Crowds of people are standing around, passionately arguing philosophy and social theories.

Lev's already sitting at our table when I walk in for supper.

"Hi there," I say, surprised to see him. I thought "goodbye" meant *goodbye*.

"I spoke to the rabbi last week," he says abruptly. "I got some perspective."

"All right . . ."

"Here's the thing. I know we're too young. I know we come from completely different worlds. But one of these days, somehow, we're going to get out of here—and we both know there's no one left. Other than running a printing press, I don't know how to do anything I *should* have learned by now; I only know how to . . . not die. You think you're going to go to conservatory? How? Do you know how to apply to one? Find an apartment? Open a bank account? Even cook a meal? I don't."

"No. I don't, either. . . ."

"I've been searching, writing to relief agencies, looking for *someone*. Family. Anyone I can ask these questions to. And no one's left, Gerta. They're all gone. I can't wait around for the perfect Kielce girl to come along, because they're all dead. The only thing to ask is, *Which way is forward?* We've *got* to go out there, and I don't want to go alone. Do you?"

"You're hoping I'll come around and be this certain kind of person."

"I'm hoping you'll be *you*, and let me be me. We can still be ourselves. Just *together*. Maybe we'll even realize we have some ways in common. I'm willing to see anything as a miracle."

"Lev, I can't talk about this anymore. You've got to stop with this pressure. I'm still with Michah. I'm leaving with him. He's right—there's nothing for me here. He's *my* way forward."

"All right, Gerta," he concedes. "I understand. He's what you always imagined. Just ask yourself one thing."

"What's that?"

"Maybe he was right for the *old* Gerta," he says, rising to leave. "But you're not the same girl I met a year ago. Maybe that person is gone. Maybe—just think about it—maybe the new Gerta is emerging. Just like your butterfly."

He slides a letter in front of me on the table and disappears into the crowd of lecture-goers.

———

My walk home after dinner is so slow, I can see the stars rotate in the night sky. Lev has this way of talking about these things—stars, futures—it resonates within me like music. *Why?* Why does he seem to know me better than I know myself? But I shake it off. It's too close. He assumes too much. He assumes I *want* him.

Gerta,

    I overstep all of my own boundaries when I'm with you. Seeing you pass the shop every day has made me hungry. All I've felt these past few years has been metal, splinter, dirty straw. The only flesh I touched was dead flesh. The only touch I received came as a beating.

    But your face—it was so soft. I felt the warmth of blood rush to your cheek, the fine structure of your jaw, like a bird's light bones. The heavy ground peeled away underneath my feet, and air came back into my lungs. When I walked away, I realized that was the first time I had cried in years.

    I won't cross the line again, but I have no regret—except to think I pushed you further away.

Lev

CHAPTER 31

Every day I take the same route: out of my bunk hall to the main road, flanked with poplar trees; past the dining hall to grab an afternoon piece of bread and an apple; around the left side of the medical building, where the print shop is. I try not to turn my head toward where I know Lev is working, but I can't help sneaking a glance just to make sure he's there. It's been a week since that last letter, and the days feel empty without them to look forward to.

Michah works in the building across from the shop, doing odd jobs. I wave at him, and he comes out and pulls me aside for a quick kiss—I know Lev can see me through the window—and then I walk past a few more buildings to the meeting hall for orchestra practice. It's become nothing more than a routine. There is no luster on it anymore. Plans for Palestine don't seem to be moving forward. And though my lips meet Michah's every day, I never hear my name pass through his.

But something new has appeared on my way. A crew of villagers is brought in to work, alongside the DPs, on a building project near the stream. This is unusual—now that most of us are feeling well and strong, we *want* to do the work ourselves, because there's a big push by those who want to leave for Palestine to learn skills they can use there. What could warrant the need to bring in outside help?

A woman and I stand watching together. Her hair is covered and she is wiping away tears. "What are they building?" I ask.

"It is a mikvah," she says in a French accent. "Didn't you know? I thought they announced it."

"I don't know what you're talking about," I say. "I've never heard that word before."

She seems shocked. "A mikvah—you know, the bath? For purity? There are so many weddings, one of the rabbis here convinced the British to help engineer one. And now they have brought Germans in to help dig it. Imagine. . . ."

"But I still don't understand," I say. "What is it for?"

"Every month, if you are married, you go to the bath after you finish your cycle. I used to run a mikvah back in France. Are you married—what is your name?"

"Gerta. No. I'm not." I chuckle. "I'm only seventeen."

"That's nothing here," she says. "Well, when you are ready, make sure to come and immerse. It is such a beautiful tradition. I can't believe we have it back." Her voice trembles.

"Oh, no, I'm not going to get married. And I—I'm not really Jewish enough to do that kind of thing anyway. I mean, I'm not religious."

She turns to me with a look of great pity. "'Gerta,' you said, yes? What do you mean, not Jewish enough? I daresay you were Jewish enough to wind up here."

"That's true," I explain, "but I'm a *musician* first."

She nods. "Oh. What do you play?"

For some reason, I trust her. "I play viola . . . but I'm *really* a singer."

"That's not really what you *are*," she says frankly.

Her directness startles me. "What do you mean?"

"It may be what you *do*. But even a voice can be taken from you."

If she only knew.

"Think of our families," she continues. "*Their* voices are silenced, but their memory lives in us, no? Something lives far below the surface—the essence of *you*. That is what remains."

"What does that have to do with . . . a bath?"

She ponders how to answer.

"I'm Hélène," she says, holding out her hand. "I stay in the barracks behind the kindergarten—by that huge sycamore tree that all of the children climb."

"Yes, I know it."

"Why don't you stop by sometime, and we can talk? When the mikvah is completed, I will show it to you. Maybe you will think better of it then."

"Thank you," I say. "I'll keep it in mind. Nice to meet you, Hélène."

"A pleasure, Gerta. *À bientôt*."

I continue on my way. She remains, watching Jews and Germans digging together.

Suddenly a memory comes back to me—something I hadn't thought about since I was little—of my mother reaching into the wooden chest at the foot of her bed and taking out a tiny book, wrapped in white tissue. I remember her reading from it, whispering rhythmically in a language I didn't understand.

I can't stop thinking about what Hélène said. What is it about me that runs deeper than voice? Than ideas? Than blood?

CHAPTER 32

It is two in the morning, a week later, and I bolt awake from a dream of end-less running and falling. All of a sudden, I just want *out* of this camp. I don't want any more questions about who I am, or am not. Michah can get me out of here, and when I get to Palestine, I'll be truly free. My Carissimi and me, letting a new life open out before us.

I run to his tent, practically still dreaming.

"Michah," I whisper-shout, flinging aside the tent flap and ducking in. "Are you in here?"

He bounds up to a sitting position on his cot, his body silhouetted against the moonlight.

"Yes—who is that? Who's there?"

"It's me, Gerta."

"Who?"

"Gerta!" I try to whisper louder. Maybe he didn't recognize my voice this quiet. "My mind's made up. I'm going to Palestine with you. You're right. There's nothing for me h—"

A groan rises from the bed as another figure turns over and reaches a slender hand toward Michah's shadow. The violin-like profile is that of a girl's hips.

"Mmm . . . darling," she moans. "Not now. No business now. Tell her to come back in the morning."

I see with complete clarity:

She is me.

Within a matter of months—maybe weeks—*I* would be in Michah's bed, getting annoyed at his new recruits, especially the pretty ones. My focus shifts from the forms of Michah and the girl, and I notice the mound of their discarded clothes, scattered paper bits, maps full of pinholes. A pistol is carelessly tossed beside a cold, unlit lantern. Michah shrinks; he's just a boy in a man's body, no more certain of the future than I am.

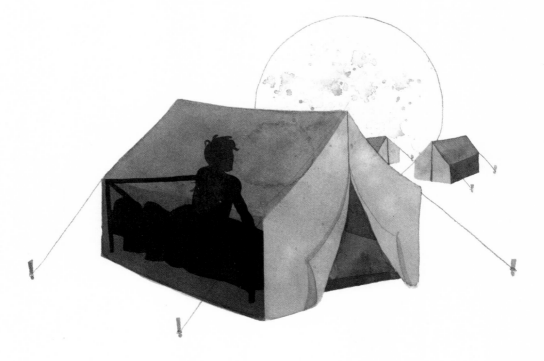

I thought I was in charge of this. I thought I could pick him up and put him down when it suited me. But this was never what I wanted. He was never interested in my music, or me. I'd be following him around, waiting for him to give me my next move.

"Never mind," I say, backing out of the tent. It is the last time I'll let my eyes turn in his direction. Michah, like Palestine, is a closed door.

CHAPTER 33

I run back toward my barracks. Even in the middle of the night, there are women at the new mikvah. They emerge as from a chrysalis, silently, their faces turned up toward the bright moon. They may walk back to their quarters with a friend, but they say nothing on the way.

I sit on the bench across from the building; it's dark enough to let my tears fall. Everything is in shambles. Someone approaches silently and sits down next to me, and I try to blot my eyes with my sleeve.

"Hello, Gerta. I was hoping I would find you here some evening. It's quite late."

"Good evening, Hélène." We have remembered each other's names. She puts her hand on my shoulder. I try to resist the urge to fall into her arms like a little girl.

"Gerta, I have been thinking about you. I wonder how many other girls are walking in your shoes. So young, coming of age with no family, no sense of who you are. You keep to yourself, not wanting to lose anything more, not knowing what's next. Is that right?"

"No, I'm fine. I'm all right." I sniff and look away, toward the clustered stars.

"Well, that may be so. But I would like to do something for you. It is not typically done for an unmarried girl. But I think it would help you. I would like to help you immerse in the mikvah."

"But—I told you. I'm not religious. And I'm not married, not planning to be. Ever." Why can't I control these stupid tears?

Hélène breathes deeply, slowly. "Come with me, Gerta."

She takes my hand—I don't resist—and leads me inside. No one is in this room at the moment, though I can hear two watery, echoing voices speaking rhythmically in the next. In the large mirror on the wall, the red rings encircling my eyes give me away, but Hélène doesn't mention it.

She listens for the voices to become silent. A lady in a robe comes back into this room, dresses behind a curtain, and greets us as she goes back out into the darkness.

"She was the last one for the evening. I'll dismiss the attendant. It'll just be us."

I'm reluctant, but I accept. Before I go in, I shower in warm water and wash away the mortification of finding Michah with that girl. I step out, realizing this is the first time I've seen my whole self in a mirror since I was fourteen.

I hardly recognize this girl.

This is the body that almost starved, that was ravaged by typhus. These are the breasts that barely developed before falling flat into my ribs. I raise my hand to my face: these are the lips that have been selfishly kissed by one boy; this is the cheek that has been tenderly caressed by another. This is who I am, Gerta Rausch. This is the body I almost gave away.

Hélène takes me into the next room and faces away as I unwrap my towel. The room is small, tiled white with a border of tiny blue mosaics. It's the most pristine place I've been to in years—since the children's choir sang for the Dutch queen in that marble and gold-leafed hall. I step into the small pool.

"You will immerse once, then twice," she instructs me. "Make sure you go completely under, including your hair. Go slow. Take your time. Call anything to mind that you want to wash away."

I release my muscles and sink down into the collected rainwater. *Call to mind what I want to be washed away?* If I did that, I would never come up; I would drown under it all. My papa limping toward the chimney. Maria standing in the doorway, watching us being arrested. The baby being thrown against the wall, the guards laughing, the crumpling mother. I dart up to the surface and shake off these thoughts.

"All right. Now repeat this prayer after me, and go under again. This time, welcome holiness upon you."

I plunge under again. Something comes over me this time. Instead of water, I feel arms surrounding me. I open my eyes. Before me is the butterfly, flapping its blue wings through the current.

CHAPTER 34

Roza and I have just finished playing for a wedding here in the concert hall. It's a beautiful evening, almost June now, and the wedding party files back to the dining hall for their reception just as the sun is setting. Roza's playing a line from this American song we love:

> To think that we were strangers a couple of nights ago,
> And though it's a dream, I never dreamed he'd ever say hello.
> Oh, maybe tonight I'll hold him tight when the moonbeams
>   shine;
> My dreams are getting better all the time.

We used to sing that kind of song in Auschwitz to remind ourselves of the world outside, where people fell in love, held each other, made plans for the future.

In a strange contrast to the wedding party that's just left, out by the side window a woman begins to wail, "My babies, my babies," as the realization finally overcomes her, so many months too late. Roza doesn't look up, but keeps playing. There's nothing to be said or done for the mother anyway. There are no words in this part of the song, so she hums instead. I sit next to her on the piano bench and harmonize.

"Sing for me, Gerta," says Roza, still playing the hopeful song. "Take the melody. Come on."

"No, no. I . . . can't."

"I don't understand," she says, and stops playing. "Help me see this from your point of view. You had a dream *and* the voice to be a singer—a great singer. I just can't see *why*—"

"Why do you think?" I'm not sure I know why myself.

"Did it do something, the starving? To your vocal cords?"

"That's part of it, yes."

"But practice will heal that. I'm getting my fingering back pretty well. The muscles will get stronger. It's just that you don't even *try*."

"No."

"Gerta. Come on. Stop this now. Are you really going to let them do this to you?"

"They took my voice." I glare at her. "I have nothing to sing for."

"No. *No.* That isn't true. Don't let them have that victory. Don't you *dare!*" Roza almost chokes on her admonition.

I can't sit here and listen to this. I go to the wings and grip the heavy green velvet curtain until I feel the fibers crush in my fist.

"You know that feeling you get when you're playing," I say after a while, "and you lose yourself in that . . . that still lake, that warmth, and you kind of . . . cease to exist?"

She nods hesitantly. "I mean, kind of . . . no, not really."

"Well, what do you think, Roza? That I can ever feel that free again? Every time a note rises in my throat, I smell that sick smoke in the air, and my chest gets so tight, because I got used to holding my breath so the ash and fever couldn't get in."

She's quiet for a while. "I know what you mean," she finally says. "Every time I look down at my hands, I'll always see them being crushed."

"But at least when I play my father's instrument, at least there's—there's his presence. I don't have to think about my own . . . existence. I feel *his* hands instead. Someday I'll run out of his rosin, I'll have to rehair the bow—but the wood always has him in it. I'd rather have that than try to sing from some-place dry and dead and empty."

"I understand." She starts playing the song again and humming.

The last sparrows of the day congregate outside the window. A man with a tuft of white hair comes and stands next to the grieving mother. He has a piece of bread, and he rips it and gives half to the woman. They tear the bread into tiny pieces and roll them between their fingers into fine crumbs, tossing them to the peeping birds. Amazing, to have a piece of bread to share with birds. The man is a millionaire.

"Gerta," Roza says, "there's this Chopin piece my mother used to play. She wasn't a fantastic player, just an amateur like me, but when she played *this* piece, it would just devastate you. She told me once, 'Roza, some things you do out of skill; some out of excitement. But some things you do out of brokenness.'"

I look down at my own hands. I remember when they were like the hands of the dead, almost. But I'm not dead. I did the work of staying alive, and that's an accomplishment. This is the time to live.

I clear my throat. "Do you know 'Ich bin der Welt abhanden gekommen'?"

"Umm . . . no . . . oh, wait, Mahler, right? I think I can plink it out if you don't mind it being . . . you know, spare."

"You'll catch on." I wink at her. I start a cappella. My throat is tight; my tongue is dry and tastes bitter. But I sing.

> *Ich bin gestorben dem Weltgetümmel,*
> *Und ruh' in einem stillen Gebiet!*
> *Ich leb' allein in meinem Himmel,*
> *In meinem Lieben, in meinem Lied.*
> I am dead to the world's tumult,
> And I rest in a quiet realm!
> I live alone in my heaven,
> In my love and in my song.

When I'm done, Roza holds the last chord as long as the piano will sustain.

"Oh, Gerta," she says. "It's not gone. It's just different."

Outside, the sky grows dark and it's getting hard to see. I go and turn on a light over the stage. Back near the door, a shadowed figure tucks quickly into the dark corner of the vestibule.

CHAPTER 35

Roza and I start playing as a sort of roving duet at all the weddings in Bergen-Belsen. Sometimes I even sing, but just harmonies for Roza. Still, I feel my voice loosening up more and more. We're getting popular. Our patrons pay us in chocolate and cigarettes. The cigarettes we trade. The chocolate is for us.

The few poor rabbis are stretched for time. Wedding announcements—and now birth announcements—take up several pages in the back of *Unzer Sztyme*. But the weddings are such a mixture of emotions. There are no fathers to ask for permission, no mothers-in-law to impress. Big sisters, grandfathers, adorable toddlers who might want to stand near the radiance of the Queen Bride—gone. Brides and grooms must give *themselves* away on the invitations.

New friendships are blooming out of the wedding preparations, though. Everywhere I look, there are little circles of women stitching, making the most precious things they can out of scraps of material. You would never know they had such meager beginnings, these veils, bow ties, even wedding rings braided from machine wire.

Lately, the talk of the camp is of a certain gown that's making the rounds. Not content to show up under the canopy wearing her charity clothes, one particular bride-to-be had her fiancé barter cigarettes with a soldier for his old parachute, which had the perfect drape for a gown. It turned out to be such a great dress, and the only one of its kind in the camp, that bride after bride—whether she's fifteen or fifty—gets in line to borrow it. Each one adds her own flair to it—a brooch, a colored sash—but underneath we all know it's The Dress.

Herr Butterman of the camp Central Committee comes to rehearsal today with some news. The Hannover Orchestra will be visiting the camp to give us a concert, and they want our musical society to play with them.

"They say that Marschner will play," he says. "We'll make it an evening to remember!"

Wolfgang Marschner, the prodigy. At nineteen—not much older than me—he's already the concertmaster of the Hannover Orchestra.

I have an idea. I run to Herr Butterman as he is turning to leave. "Please, sir, would you be able to send a message to the conductor? How would I go about that?"

"Just write it down, dear, and I'll make sure it goes where it needs to go," he says.

I grab a piece of manuscript paper and try my best to remember what I learned in school about writing a formal letter.

Herr Direktor,

    Gerta Rausch (Richter), former student of Koloratursopran Maria Büchner and daughter of violist Klemens Richter, would like to inquire of the Maestro whether he would permit her to sing "Erbarme dich" from the St. Matthew Passion, which was to have been her debut before her deportation from Würzburg. She still has the score in her possession. Kindly write with your thoughts on the matter.

                Gratefully,

                GR, Bergen-Belsen DP Camp

"I'll see what I can do," says Herr Butterman, a bittersweet smile tempering the excitement he wore when he made the announcement. I feel only a little guilt over using Maria Büchner's name to obtain a favor. *She owes it to me*, I think with self-satisfaction.

Two days later, Herr Butterman finds me at the piano, leaning on the music stand with my left arm and plucking out the melody from "Erbarme dich" with my right.

"Miss Rausch," he says, "I have good news for you." He hands me an envelope. "You will make your long-overdue debut."

CHAPTER 36

It's the big day. For two weeks, I've done nothing but sleep, eat and rehearse for my debut. The orchestra arrives, and I await them by the door of the rehearsal room as they load in their instruments and hang their hats. I'm tingling and restless, excited to rehearse and perform with a real, professional orchestra. All of my childhood memories rush in: I'm standing in the wings, watching Papa take his viola from the case, rosin the bow and begin to tune among the chatter, the dinner plans, the gossip.

The double basses and timpani are rolled in, and helping to wheel in a harp is a woman with a turquoise scarf over blond hair, wearing sunglasses and deep red lipstick. As she is about to pass me, she stops suddenly. Slowly she takes off her glasses.

It is Maria Büchner.

"Gerta! I—" She is speechless. She stares at me. I feel a rage begin to well up inside me, and I want to hit her. I want to tear out her hair. I want to smash her with all of the betrayal I feel afresh as I breathe in that damn gardenia perfume. She comes toward me with her gloved hand outstretched, her mouth open and trembling, her eyes wide. She looks simultaneously ashamed and full of tenderness. All of a sudden, she peels off her gloves, letting them drop to the floor, and begins patting my face, as uncontrollable sobs take over her whole body. She actually falls to the ground in a heap.

"I couldn't find you. I couldn't find you!" she says, over and over again. "I tried, but I couldn't find you."

It disgusts me, this effervescent and very public show of—what? Repentance? The useless assertion that she "tried"? What am I to do with this mess of tears and rouge at my feet? Absolve her of the death of my father? Of the loss of my innocence?

Here is Maria Büchner, at my feet.

The picture in my head, for three years now, has been this: her watching us being marched to the end of the street, spinning on her heel back into the house, closing and locking the door. Maybe she had a glass of wine, took our photographs off the mantel, listened to a record of Gershwin before taking off her dressing gown and getting back into her feather-and-down bed, shedding nary a tear, moving on to the next unattached man, the next starstruck little girl.

"Forgive me. My daughter. Forgive me."

My daughter.

I see a string of moments:

Maria and me dancing together, singing the melody to Bach's "Wachet auf" chorale while Papa plays the motif.

Lying with Maria under her pillowy comforter patterned with red and pink roses, her unpinned hair falling over me while I recover from a nightmare.

Standing onstage in the empty concert hall in Würzburg, learning how to tease the loudest voice out of my belly while Maria stands in the back row of the balcony. "More!" she demands. "Make me weep from a hundred kilometers away!"

Was I wrong? She is human, ordinary. She may have even suffered. Maybe she really *is* sorry. Crouching down, I want to reach out to her, but my mind is on fire. She lifts her head and strokes my cheek.

"Gerta. *Mein Herzchen*." We rise together. She folds me in an embrace that I cannot bring myself to return. I don't know how she can face me after what she's done.

"I hate you, Maria," I whisper in her ear. My eyes are hot, my mouth full of spit. "I hate you."

"I know," she says plainly. "You should."

Marschner's performance of the Brahms Violin Concerto is transcendent. At least compared to the music we have been making in our little musical society. Together with the Hannover Orchestra, we've decided on four selections from Bach's *St. Matthew Passion*. The choir files into the sliver of stage behind the orchestra, and I take a chair next to the first violin, to the supportive applause of my fellow DPs and the tapping feet of my orchestra mates, who, until we began these rehearsals, never knew I sang. The conductor lifts his baton, and I'm invigorated hearing the familiar passages: the drone of the double bass as the heartrending introduction begins, the strings peeling away layers like birch bark.

The voices begin:

> *Kommt, ihr Töchter, helft mir klagen—*
> Come, daughters, help me lament—

It's time. Marschner's solo line plays the opening of "Erbarme dich." I feel no hint of nervousness. As soon as the first note comes out of my mouth, though, I worry. My voice sounds squeaky, strained:

> *Erbarme dich, mein Gott,*
> *Um meiner Zähren Willen!*
> Have mercy, my God,
> On my iron will!

Maria stands in the wings, chewing her lip. The audience is a vast, dark field of unpredictable creatures moving and fidgeting. All I can feel is judgment, not the freedom I was expecting, the release of all this pent-up breath.

Since the Nazis took us, I've spent every minute trying to be invisible, to become smaller to avoid beatings, hiding in the safety of being last-chair viola. What made me think I was ready for this?

And that is it. I seize up completely. I can't remember a single additional lyric.

I am caught. Discovered. Nothing I thought about myself is true: I am a fraud. Frozen and shrinking, I stand stunned onstage until the orchestra has finished the piece, Marschner coming to my aid and playing the melody I should be singing. At last—at long last—the piece ends, and I walk off with as much dignity as I can manage.

CHAPTER 37

The chairs are folded and moved against the wall. Tables are furnished with treats unseen since before the war. The hunger of the people is a force of its own, and they practically climb on Marschner to touch the edge of his jacket—not just because of his celebrity, but because *art* entered with him through the gates of Bergen-Belsen.

I press myself into the farthest corner of the wings, wanting to dissolve into the wall and forget that I ever opened my mouth tonight. Someone is coming toward me, and before I open my clenched eyes to see, I know who it is.

"Gerta," Maria whispers, "are you all right? Why not come out and have something to eat?"

A sideways glance at her unleashes a stream of tears I didn't even know stood in my eyes. She embraces me. I have no choice but to melt into her arms, and I heave and gasp.

"My love, *mein Liebling*," she whispers, and lets me cry. "My love."

I sink to the floor, and she descends with me. I cry myself to exhaustion.

"I didn't betray you, you know," she says, stroking my hair. I pull away and look at her. Her face is calm. "I know you must have wondered. I can feel it when I hold you. But I promise, I never could have done that. You were my Gertalein. Child of my heart." Maria takes a deep breath. "God, that was the worst day of my life. . . . I thought if I just played along . . ."

She sighs and readies herself to tell me the story. "After they took you away, I was standing there, just staring, thinking about who I could speak to, bribe, anything I could do to save you and Klemens. Not five minutes later, another squad showed up, this time the Hitler Youth. *Kids*. Like you. They pushed past me into the house and took *everything*. They dragged me out and took me to the police station and . . . well, you don't need to know that. The next morning, they took me out to the Residenz square. One of the Hitler Youth put a sign around my neck and told me that they had taken our home as a fine for my being a 'Jew lover.' And I was, Gerta. I loved your father. And I will never apologize for loving that great, gentle man."

My chest aches, thinking I could have blamed Maria.

"He loved you, too," I reassure her. "I know he did."

We stare across the stage. "It was Rudolf. Your father's student."

I sit back hard against the wooden wall. *"Rudolf?"*

"He put the sign around my neck himself."

The realization dawns. "So that's why he stopped coming. The Hitler Youth."

"Your father was returning from a concert one night when the first deportation crossed right in front of him. He saw Rudolf there, in the uniform. From that point on, we could see what was coming—there was only so long before they caught on to your fake *Ahnenpass*. We tried to leave the country, but it was impossible. The tighter we felt the noose, the more we threw ourselves into music—for your sake. We tried not to pass our fear on to you. We wanted to keep you innocent and free. But we also wanted you to have a skill you could take with you, so you could feel capable. That's why I tried to teach you charm as well. It's a form of diplomacy. And you did it, Gerta. You absorbed the instincts we hoped for you. Do you see?"

"I think so." My throat tightens, thinking of Papa standing by the window, chewing his pipe.

"I want you to understand something, Gerta. No one starts operatic technique at fourteen—that's ludicrous. Yes, there are those rare prodigies, but they're mostly parroting. The voice has only one ally: *time*. Age and experience are king. They ripen you—not just your voice, but you. You lived, Gertalein, thank God. You're young. You have time ahead of you to heal. There is a deepening ahead. Don't think about tonight. Get right back onstage the very next chance you get."

"I will, Maestra. I promise." Soberly, I tuck my arm under hers and lean on her shoulder. We're quiet for a while.

"How did you end up in Hannover?" I ask.

"Marschner contacted me about your letter. I've been staying with friends since I was evicted, living from place to place, concert to concert. Everywhere I went, I tried to follow a thread, some clue to find you. This time I got lucky. It's just been me and this bag of clothes. And these. I would have given them to you before you went onstage, but I didn't think you'd receive them from me until you knew the whole story."

She takes out a paper package. Inside—the green taffeta gown, and a framed photo of the three of us by the lake at Bad Windsheim.

I look at her, knowing the truth. "There never was going to be a debut, was there?"

"No, Gerta. There never was a debut."

It all makes sense. Maria giving me her clothes. Papa stuffing the good viola case with rosin and strings. Always catching Anna Müller humming my solo. The ceaseless training, even too young. They were trying to give me options. And hope.

"Gerta, you will leave here soon, don't worry. You'll start your life. You'll even be happy, sometimes. And I'd . . . like to be part of that."

"How?"

"Come home with me. We can be a family again. We don't have to stay in Hannover; we can go wherever we want, find a good conservatory for you. It doesn't have to be in Germany. We can go to Vienna, New York. . . . I still know some people."

It's tempting. I loved Maria. I still do. But too much has happened. There's no going back. Now that I know the truth, I think I could sit and laugh with her in her apartment, but only as a guest.

"No," I say, wavering, "no, I don't think so, Maria."

She looks at me with a stoic woundedness. "I understand. Here, then. Take this so you know how to find me. In case you need anything. Or you want to write."

She writes her address on the concert program. I press my cheek to hers and breathe deeply before I get up to go.

"Wait," she calls after me. "There's one more thing."

I turn back. "What is it?"

She hesitates. "Your father . . . he had a sister."

My ears ring. Can it be true?

"Is she . . . alive?"

"Her name is Ruth," she says, reaching into her bag. She hands me a crumpled envelope. "She's a psychologist. She lives in Palestine, in one of those communes. If you wrote to her, she might be able to sponsor you to go there."

I have an aunt. Suddenly the world is open. Everything is mine. I bend down and kiss Maria's cheek and squeeze her hand. She stays sitting on the floor, watching me leave.

I run grinning into the night and hear a commotion in a distant field. It's yet another wedding. The bride and groom, lifted on chairs, hold each end of a scarf across a tarp wall stretched between stakes, and it waves in a breeze made by dancing men on one side, dancing women on the other. The couple's eyes are fixed on each other as they undulate on this sea of strangers, this sea of brethren. I'm mesmerized. A burst of laughter from the party startles me, and I keep running back to my room.

Waiting on my pillow is a letter. I don't want to open it—the world is too good right now without Lev's prolonged goodbyes. I hold the sealed letter as I kick off my shoes. I don't let it go even as I get out of my dress and under the covers in my slip. Lying in bed, drifting to sleep, I finally open the letter.

Gerta,

Someday, when you are on the other side of the world, watching your dreams play out before you, I hope you'll think of me and maybe drop me a line. Only tell me the happy parts, if you want. I love—even from far away, even for someone else—to see the smile returning to your face, to hear that music wanting to burst from you. Let it. Let the joy come peeking through where it wants, when it wants.

> *Always yours,*
> *Lev*

CHAPTER 38

The morning is already so hot, I'm up before the sun appears over the tree-tops. All night I sweated in my bed, the thin mattress offering no buffer for my constant tossing and turning. I dreamed of Lev, though I don't remember what happened. I only remember that I woke up smiling.

Outside, it's cooler; while I can get a breath of lighter air, I take a walk toward the meadow path again. The camp is quiet except for some early sounds—dishwater sloshing in pots behind the dining hall, the cry of a baby who rose earlier than his mother would have preferred. I pass the mikvah, shut and silent until nightfall, when the women will come. There is Michah's tent; God knows who is waking up with him this morning.

A metallic rhythm grows louder as I walk, exactly like the sound of a train on tracks.

The sound comes from the open door of the print shop. Through the big windows, I watch the week's edition of *Unzer Sztyme* rolling over the cylinders of the press. In the corner, the spidery arms of another small press crawl over a stack of leaflets printed in Hebrew. I'm not sure I realized how early

Lev starts work. He stands in front of a tabletop divided into compartments, placing tiny rectangular prisms of leaden letterforms into a bracket in his hand. How quickly his careful hand moves, weaving lines of type, working backward.

He looks up and sees me standing, transfixed, in the doorway. Our eyes meet, and all of a sudden I remember to breathe. I lift my hand in a tentative wave. He smiles and holds up a finger, telling me to wait a moment. He finishes his block of type and walks toward me, wiping his hands on his apron.

"Good morning," he says.

"Hello, Lev," I say. "How are you?"

"Well. I'm well. It's early for a musician to be up, no?"

"It's the heat," I say, tugging my collar. "I couldn't stay asleep."

"Yes, I know it. These machines don't help," says Lev, sweat beading around his eyes. He pulls a handkerchief from his apron pocket and wipes his face.

"I enjoyed the performance last night," he says.

"You were there?" I cringe. "Oh, I'm sorry you had to see that."

"Of course I was there. I felt for you. I could never stand in front of a crowd like that."

"It never used to bother me before. I wasn't even nervous last night. Something just . . . happened. I couldn't remember a single word."

"Don't worry. It'll come. And I enjoyed the ten seconds I heard," he teases. The way Lev's eyes twinkle reminds me of Papa's smiling eyes, Maria's raspy laugh, the harmonies of choir children.

"I got your letter last night," I say. "You have a way with words, you know."

He starts untying his denim work apron. "Maybe I say too much."

"No," I assure him. "I love reading your letters. I missed them."

"They're nothing," he says, "just my own particulars."

"That's not nothing," I say. "You should write a book."

"Me?" He gestures toward the boxes of alphabets. "No, no. I just run the press for *other* people's words."

"I think you underestimate yourself, Lev—your writing. You're *good* at it." He doesn't answer me, but this wistful look comes over his face. A bead of sweat runs down his neck. The heat in the shop grows overwhelming, so we walk out to find breeze and shade. We sit on a half wall just outside, under a great tree marked by bullets.

"Lev," I begin, "I'm leaving."

"Leaving? Where? How?"

"Palestine."

Lev is quiet for a moment. He meets my eyes with an intensity I haven't seen in him before. "Palestine, then?"

"That's right."

"I see," says Lev, looking down at his stained hands and picking at dried ink under his thumbnail.

"I have a chance to start over completely," I say.

"Ah. Well, I hope you'll be very happy together. Really, Gerta, mazel tov. I wish you the very best."

I'm confused at first. What could he be talking about?

"Oh! Oh. Lev, you can't think—no. Did you think I was talking about Michah? That's over. It wasn't what I thought it was."

"Oh?" He tilts his head, purses his lips.

"No! I have an aunt I never knew about, on a kibbutz."

"That's wonderful! Family!" He seems intensely relieved. "Ah—but Gerta on a kibbutz, tending farm." He grins. "That's a picture."

I play along. "I can't remember. Do potatoes grow on trees or vines?"

"I don't think they grow potatoes in the desert, my friend!" It feels so good to laugh with him.

"Will you be able to sing?" Lev asks. "Are there opera houses there?"

"There's Tel Aviv."

"Right. Tel Aviv. That's far away." He rolls his sleeves up higher. We sit there in silence for a whole minute. I can hear him take short breaths, like he's about to speak but keeps changing his mind.

"Lev." I turn toward him, forcing him to look at me. "You want to say something. It's all right. If we're going to say goodbye, let's be honest with each other."

"All right." He sighs hard. "I don't want you to go. Because—how do I say this—you know that feeling you get when you're singing, Gerta, and you lose yourself in a still lake, and there's this warmth, and you kind of . . . cease to exist . . ."

"What—"

"The way I love you, Gerta, it's like that. It's like music. It's like praying."

The leaves shimmer in the heat, and the chitter of cicadas rises across the field.

"I won't lie," he continues."Being friends with you . . . it's painful. I've tried to think of every way in the world to win you over. But there's this certain picture you have in mind, and I'm not in it. I know."

"But, Lev—" I start, though I have no idea what to say next.

"The thing is, you've made things very clear for me."

"Me?" I'm astonished. "How? All I've done is confuse things."

"No, no." He stands suddenly. "You let me be myself. You listened. You didn't try to make me into someone else. That's another kind of freedom, to have a patient friend who lets you get to the bottom of who you really are."

I look down at my shoes. Even outside the print shop, I breathe in the acrid smell of ink settling on the print rollers. The machines have stilled now, but soon, the drums will be turning and printing the news of another, competing paper.

Lev is saying something, but I'm somewhere else, and I can't make out the words, just the last bit—

"You made me feel . . . joy."

My head feels unlidded, too light. Between my shoulders my heart squeezes, as though some doctor were massaging it to life. My voice fills my throat. Not until I lift my head do I realize what I've been running from.

He's turned to walk back to the shop. "Wait," I call.

He stops in the doorway. "Gerta, it's all right. I didn't tell you—I'm leaving soon as well. Back to Kielce, to see if there's anyone left. I got a temporary pass for a few days. Don't worry. I won't be stuck here for long."

"Wait. Lev—" I run to him and stop just inches from his face. Here are his eyes again, worlds within worlds, the road opening before both of us. In his eyes, I see and am truly seen.

It's Lev.

It's always been Lev.

"Gerta, I can't be this close to you." His eyes are full of pain. "Please."

"What was it you once said, Lev?" I whisper. "When love comes up alongside you . . . it's best to take a walk with it."

We are married in our grove a week later, under the chuppah at twilight. The poles are adorned with budding branches and held by Lev's fellow news-papermen. He has covered my face with an opaque veil. I can't see what lies before me, and I must trust Maria and Hélène, standing on either side, to walk me to the canopy. They lead me in procession around Lev, weaving a fortress that only I will enter.

One of the other violists plays a solemn melody on Papa's viola. I ache for my father to bless me; I hear Lev weeping, speaking the names of everyone who should be here but is not.

We make our promises over a brimming cup of red wine and drink deeply from it. Lev crushes a glass wrapped in cloth under his foot; in this one moment, we live years of destruction and joy, past and future.

I am the fifteenth girl to get married in this dress, made from a soldier's parachute.

CHAPTER 39

The girls from my barracks have made this little side room into a bridal suite, with glasses and teapots full of flowers. Hélène has crocheted us a lacy bedspread. It's all so pretty—and I'm so scared.

I'm not sure what I ever pictured about losing my virginity. The truth is that I didn't really *ever* picture it, even with Michah. There was the time Maria told me how babies get made. But that was all wrapped up in the emergency with my nightgown. I was such a child then, and it was only three years ago. All I know is that Lev and I are just supposed to take off our clothes and figure it out.

"Gerta?" Lev is standing by the window. He's just pulled the curtains closed and taken off his hat and jacket.

"Huh?" I've still got my hand on the doorknob. I haven't blinked in a whole minute. "I don't . . . feel well."

"Let's sit down. Come here." Lev pours me a glass of water from the pitcher on the bedside table.

"Do you know what you're doing?" I ask. "How this is supposed to . . . work?"

"Well, the rabbi told me a little . . . but I'm pretty sure we'll know what to—"

"What have we done?" I'm starting to panic. "I just didn't think about this being part of it."

"You *didn't*?"

"Well . . . no. 'Friends for life,' remember?"

Lev's shoulders sink. I know this was supposed to be a magical night. But the last time I had to undress in front of someone, there were guns and dogs, and I'm trying to remind myself: *This is not that . . . this is not that. . . .*

"Kissing!" I blurt out. "Kissing. We can start there."

"Oh!" He's suddenly heartened. "Sure! That sounds good!" He looks like he's just been told that he's inherited a fortune. He leans toward me. We're too far apart on the bed, and he doesn't even know what to do with his lips. "No," I say, putting my fingers up. "You don't stick them out like that. Here, let me show you."

I move closer and touch his nose with mine, and our lips just brush. Our eyes are open and that goofy grin spreads across his face. Just then, he loses his balance on the edge of the bed and slips, knocking a plate of heart-shaped Linzer cookies off the table with a crash. We both burst out laughing.

"I'm sorry," he says, sitting there on the floor. "I'm sorry. This is terrible."

"I love your kind of terrible." I laugh. He makes me smile, this boy I've just married. This best friend of mine. "Lev . . . Levi . . . come here." I stretch out my hand and pull him back up, and we fall into an instinctive embrace. We're suddenly quiet, lying next to each other on the pillow, so close. As long as it's like this, maybe I don't have to worry.

"You know what?" I whisper.

"What?"

"We're *married*. I'm your *wife*."

"That, Gerta Rausch, is complete insanity."

He lifts his hand and slowly, barely, runs his fingers along my face.

"You don't have that scared look in your eyes this time," I say.

"Well, I can touch you now. I don't have to apologize. Plus, I'm dreaming." He takes a lock of my hair and spins it around his fingers and then plunges them fully into my hair, and he draws me close, chest to chest. His kiss surprises me; it's assertive. It demands a response.

I give him a response.

"Gerta," Lev says softly, "can I love you now? As much as I want to?"

"More than that," I say, undoing his first button, my heart pounding. He reaches behind me and feels for the zipper of my dress. He pulls the sleeve back off my shoulder to reveal that pretty gray brassiere, to loop his finger through the strap, to rest his lips on my collarbone.

I peel back the layers and finally get to Lev's skin. There are signs of old beatings. They're significant. I kiss each part of him that was so terribly mistreated.

Nothing's hurried. It's all discovery and goose bumps and flinching at unexpectedness.

I feel the cool night air on my bare skin, the swirling in my chest. There is no shame here, no pretending. It feels . . . clean. It's like the first time I saw Lev, through fever-blurred eyes in the medical tent, and he seemed so strangely familiar. We lie there and look at each other, and it's as though I'm watching him travel through time, as he gained five kilos, ten, twenty—and here he is now, a column of sinew and muscle before me. He is somehow . . . majestic. Gloriously *alive*.

It occurs to me in this moment: I am the only one who will ever see his scars. And he is the only one who ever need see mine.

CHAPTER 40

Here is a sound:

Like a distant, rushing wind, with a bit of a whistle in it. Papa on one side, Maria on the other, comforting me from a nightmare. They have turned on the small pink bedside lamp, casting light on the photo of the three of us in our bathing suits at Bad Windsheim. My nightmare blinks away—flames, the city in flames, me and Uncle Bernard watching from the dining room window. A woman made of fire is running in and out of the buildings, a woman I used to call Mama. She has a long trail of flame-hair and is blazing toward me with her arms outstretched, calling my name—

Gerta! Gertalein! Meine Liebe, Gerta!

And the buildings burn but are not consumed. And here is the image of the Man Who Never Smiles, whose face is everywhere but whose name Papa and Maria never utter. And here is Papa crying in the night, and that sound again—

Hush . . . shh . . . shhh . . .

Between Papa and Maria and the photo by the lake.

Hush . . . shh . . . shhh . . .

But that was years ago. A childhood ago. This sound—what is it now?

I am so warm.

It is the *shhh* of the radiator hissing steam in our room, of rain on the roof. It is the sound of Lev's quiet breath on the back of my neck as I curve into his body, here on our first night as husband and wife.

CHAPTER 41

We board the train for Poland. Lev wants one more chance to find a familiar person in his hometown. It is unusually cool for early July, especially considering how hot it was just last week. I've decided to wear my head scarf, now that I'm two weeks into being an old married lady.

The train to Kielce is a normal passenger train, a strange contrast to our history on the railroad. We have actual tickets, and food in our satchel—cold meat and bread. The fields stretch out before us, green and promising. Pine trees wave as the train rushes past them. The tracks play a waltz; in my mind I hear Chopin.

"So, *wife*," Lev begins, turning to me, a kind of mischievous look in his eyes.

"Yes, *husband*?" The word seems so foreign and impossible. We're children, aren't we? Who said we could use those words?

"What are we going to do about our home?"

"You mean the room we share with ten other couples?" I say with a sarcastic smirk. "That home?"

"No, you know—doing things the Jewish way. Keeping kosher, the prayers—"

I flinch. "I thought we agreed I didn't have to be someone I'm not," I say, suddenly defensive. "Are you changing your mind?"

"No, no," he says, taking my hand. "But you're doing some of it already, like the mikvah. Do you want me to . . . help you—"

"Not now. Don't ask me that right now." I pull my hand away.

"All right, all right." He turns and looks out the window. It's disorienting how quickly we got into this fight.

A few minutes pass, the track rhythm sounding less waltz than clock, ticking out agonizing seconds of silence.

"Gerta," he says at last, "let me ask you this way: What do you want your Sabbath table to look like? When we finally have a real home."

"Look like? I don't know," I say. "What we already do. Light the candles, sing some songs, eat dinner? What else is there?"

I'm not this out of touch, really. When I awkwardly circle the candles with my hands and repeat the prayers after him, I'm aware of the transcendence of it, the bubble of unseen light that surrounds us.

"Think about it, Gerta. When you think of a time you were truly happy, the most . . . at peace, what comes to mind?" He leans his head against the seat and fiddles with the silver ring on my finger.

Of course, I know the answer. Papa and Maria by the fireplace, playing viola and piano; a warm dinner, sweet mint iced tea in my glass. But no— there's something further back. There's the shadow memory of a woman's freckled arms, and I'm young, *so* young, sucking my thumb and twirling her dark blond hair, and she is singing to me, in a different language, a different world.

I push the memory away. "That question feels . . . strangely selfish," I say.

"What?" he asks, mystified. "Why?"

"Here we are, arguing about how to rest and eat and pray . . . these little things . . . What right do we have . . ."

The fact is, these aren't little things. I don't want to admit that *home* means as much as it does. I'm afraid that if I open the door a crack, the sorrow will never leave, will grow in me like a cancer.

"So," he says, "you think it would honor our families if we went through the rest of our lives in mourning? Maybe living in an empty room? With a bare lightbulb overhead?"

"Forget it." I sigh. "Why waste any time thinking about it? I don't want to live in constant questioning. I just want to live my life. Our life."

The train slows and pulls into a station. There's the exchange of passengers. Babies cry, adjust, quiet. A pack of blond Polish boys walks through the car, laughing cruelly with menacing faces, scrutinizing people row by row. I don't understand their language, but Lev does. He sinks into his coat and turns his head toward the window. We don't speak until the train is settled again, moving through the countryside.

Lev says, after a long time, "You say you don't want to live in constant questioning. Neither do I, Gerta. But I think there's a time to wrestle and to shake your fist at the sky. And then there's the time to admit that we're not going to get any answers."

This brings up such a rage in me.

Not because I disagree. I have my own history—I've trembled with the awareness of some other presence, something, *someone*, who knows my name.

No—I rage because I ache.

"All right," I say, through a tight jaw, "what do you want *your* Sabbath table to look like?"

Lev gathers me between his strong shoulders. I lay my angry head on his chest under his red beard and listen to his voice resonate. He sighs.

"The sun's about to set. The table's laid with wine, two shiny loaves of braided bread covered with a cloth, candles in silver candlesticks. You come into the room in that dress I like and cover your head with white lace. You gather the flame toward your eyes and say the blessing. You cover your eyes with your hands and ask God for the secret desires of your heart. There are friends at the table who love us, and the weary and hungry who have come to our door. We break bread, we drink wine, we sing raucous songs. We laugh and let the cares roll off our shoulders and out the door. We say goodbye to our friends. Then you and I go to bed, and I kiss your face . . . your neck . . . your shoulders . . . and we go back to the Garden of Eden."

Raindrops begin hitting the window, spreading into soft rivulets. He's quiet; he's said all he needs to. He curls his fingers around mine and looks out at the passing fields. I don't regret saying yes to Lev. I love him. Not just because he loves me, but because he's *Lev*.

My Lev.

Whatever our table looks like, whatever we do on that day of rest or any other day, if I have music, and I have Lev, I'm home.

"You know what I want?" I sit up, willing him to see my whole heart. "I want you to just *be* there. I want you to keep the light on when the horrors come, and let me do the same for you. I want to be seventeen and in love and to sing my heart out every chance I get. And I'm not going to trade that for anything. I'm *not*."

"I'd never ask you to," he assures me.

"Because it's *you*, Lev. It's you."

CHAPTER 42

We are slowing into the Kielce station. Lev reaches overhead and takes down the viola and our modest bag with all our worldly possessions: our travel papers, a change of clothes, Lev's prayer book. On the platform are men in work caps, women in worn cotton dresses, weary grandmothers embracing grandchildren who were babies before the war. Each of them turns to look at us, some for an instant. More of them look us up and down and mutter things—"*Żyd, brudny, nieczysty*"—things like that. I don't understand Polish, but I understand voices.

Our stay in Kielce is not beginning well.

Not one taxi will stop for us, though we hail for twenty minutes. Finally, a man with a donkey cart stops. He dismounts and pulls us close to the cart. He chews on his cigarette, spits and sighs hard.

"You here for the funeral?" he asks Lev, looking askance at the fringes hanging from his waist. "It's that way. I have to hand it to you Jews—you're brave to come back. Or stupid."

"We're just here to see what's left of my family's home. What funeral? Who died?"

He stares at us. "You kids didn't know? On Planty Street, across from the park, you know, with the little stream? Forty-some Jews. Murdered. It was a bloodbath the whole day. Like they avenged the entire war on them. The police did nothing—in fact, they were in on it. How did you not hear about this?"

I feel bile rise in my mouth. I want to run back to the train, but it's already pulled away. This station with its hanging baskets of flowers is another sham, like Theresienstadt with its concerts, plays and lectures. But Lev is bargaining with the man to give us a ride, and before I can argue, he's helping me into the back of the cart.

"I heard the commissioner on the radio," the man leans back to tell us. "Get this—he said, 'The police showed incredible restraint; not a single shot was fired at the people.' I guess the ones with the police bullets in their backs weren't 'the people.' Anyway," he says, "you should know *I* never had anything to do with any of this." Lev looks at me sideways.

We have him take us the opposite direction from the funeral, staying well clear, and we arrive at a house on a corner. It is charming but a little rundown. A small garden on the side of the house seems to be growing only a trellis of neglected beans. Lev knocks at the door. A woman answers, drying her hands on her navy-blue apron. She's in her fifties, a shock of white hair in two crossed braids atop her head. She is startled at the sight of us.

"Ech! Jews! What do *you* want?" she spits.

"Good morning, ma'am," Lev says, with a slight bow of the head. I can't believe he can be civil to her. "I wonder if you can help me. You see, this was my uncle's house. I was wondering if anyone from this street surv—"

"Didn't they kill all of you?" she hollers. "How can you show your face? Get out of here! Get out!" People are watching us behind their curtains. We run down the street and turn a corner.

We will ourselves to be small and invisible as we risk approaching the vicinity of the funeral. Dozens of plain wooden coffins of all sizes lie in a trench surrounded by the small crowd, all that remains of the Jewish community of Kielce, once twenty-five thousand strong. Lev says he recognizes a few of the mourners. All of them look decades older. None of them are his relatives.

Surrounding the mourners is a ring of drunken youths shouting and laughing. They are kept at bay by a handful of uncommitted policemen. The survivors shovel the soil over the coffins and disband.

We leave ahead of them.

Lev and I stick to the side streets and small parks where the trees are dense and we can disappear into the shadows. He stuffs his tzitzit into his waistband, puts his curls under his flat cap and tucks his bearded chin into his coat collar. I take his cue and remove my head scarf. I have such a sharp vigilance in my chest that the slightest sound startles me. I'm panting from fear.

"Lev, we have to get out of here," I plead, clutching his coat. "Take me out of here! Back to the station, *please*!"

"I will, my love, but we have to do one thing first, and then I promise we'll leave—and never come back."

He grabs my hand and we walk four blocks, quick but inconspicuous, until we come to a solitary house set back into a stand of birch trees. This

time, we don't knock on the door. Instead, Lev enters the gate, counts out eighteen steps along the side of the garden and four steps toward the house, crouches down and begins to dig with his hands. My chest is so tight, I can barely breathe.

"What are you *doing*?" I whisper. He does not answer. He has dug a hole as deep as his elbow and feels around inside. He suddenly looks up, pure joy on his face. A bit more digging, and what emerges from the hole are two silver candlesticks, wrapped in a disintegrating pillowcase.

"These were my mother's," Lev says, brushing them off and tucking them into his overcoat. "Now we can go."

All the way back across the Polish countryside, from town to town, into the rubble cities of eastern Germany, we see with different eyes. People get on and off this train, hard faces caked with war and loss. Even the skinny demands to their weary parents, or they don't—can't—talk at all. Lev's learned to hide behind a newspaper when the gangs of boys get on the train. At more than one station we've seen them beating Jews on the platform, cheered by onlookers.

All these lives in ruin. I feel so small. Where can we go from here? Is there a yeshiva for Lev? Will some former Nazi give him a newspaper job? Are we up for the fight?

Bergen-Belsen's yawning fences curl us back into the den where thousands still wait in limbo for an answer to the question, *where?* We don't wait for an answer. We find Michah immediately and tell him of the massacre. He grits his teeth.

I don't recognize Michah now as someone with whom I once shared intimate space. He is simply who he came here to be; his goal, to bring Jews to safety.

"We have to go *now*, Michah," Lev demands. "How soon is the next ship leaving?"

"In three weeks," he says. "Gerta has told you how you must get there?"

"Yes. On foot. We are ready."

V

OASIS

En Route to the British Mandate of Palestine

Summer 1946–Winter 1947

CHAPTER 43

Michah slips an envelope into the hand of the British guard at the gate, nods, and we cross the threshold of Bergen-Belsen for the last time. He leads twelve of us, including Roza, across the devastated breadth of Europe. We walk for three weeks, finding the occasional respite in the barns of sympathetic villagers. It's hot, and the forest floor is overgrown. Thankfully, Lev and I have only brought one bag between us, and Papa's viola. It's all we own, and that's just fine.

We're joined by others along the way, but they split off once we grow to fifteen or so. Larger groups raise suspicion, but small cohorts like ours are constantly moving across the continent in a thousand directions. We aren't the only ones displaced by the war. A year on, everyone is still ravaged, shamed, trying to figure out why one was left and another was taken. Even the most cheerful greeting only partially hides the ubiquitous hollow stare.

It's hard to believe—here it is, August, and we're walking ankle-deep in high mountain snow somewhere in Switzerland. Michah overtakes us.

"Hey, the lovely Rausch-Goldszmits—wait a minute, will you?" Lev turns and feigns a little smile. He's grateful to Michah for smuggling us, but it's still hard for him to push away the image of Michah and me together.

"Gerta . . ." Michah almost touches my arm but thinks better of it. My name coming from his mouth is disorienting. "Can I speak to you?"

"Sure," I say, and pull aside a bit. Lev casts a doubtful look at us. "It's all right, Lev. Go ahead; I'll catch up."

Lev walks heavily up the hill, still within earshot. Michah and I hang back.

"I didn't get around to saying thanks for taking care of my mother," he says, sober in a way I've never seen him. "I'm glad she wasn't alone at the end."

"I was an orphan; she was a mother," I say. "We helped each other."

He hesitates. "I also wanted to say . . . I'm sorry."

"For what?"

"Every time I saw you, I could only think of what I had lost. It was too much. I had to forget. The truth is, it was easier to pretend no one had names, or individual faces. Just focus on the *cause*—to get as many Jews to

Palestine as I could, and that's it. The girls"—the vapor from Lev's parted lips comes faster as he overhears—"the girls just numb me. I can forget I'm actually still alive."

The snow gets into our shoes. Lev's pant cuffs are soaked; a line of sweat runs out from under the brim of his hat. A crow calls to its mate.

We come to a lookout point where we rest and take out some bread and fruit. The valley floor spreads out in a rainbow of greens below. A murmuration of starlings swirls on the air current.

"I forgive you, Michah," I eventually manage to respond, handing him a torn-off piece of bread.

We finally reach the French port, and once all the smaller groups of refugees converge, we're four thousand strong. The *Oasis* is an old boat, not built

for passengers but for small industry, its hull rusted and its wooden siding peeling off of stripped nails. Lev and I ask each other with our eyes, *Are we going to end our journey at the bottom of the Mediterranean?*

The horn blows and the *Oasis* pulls out from the dock, heading, as far as the authorities know, for Istanbul under a false flag. Despite the sun, the deck is the only tolerable place to be. The heat belowdecks is hellish with the smell of sweat and sick. The sea wind offers enough relief to let us sleep in

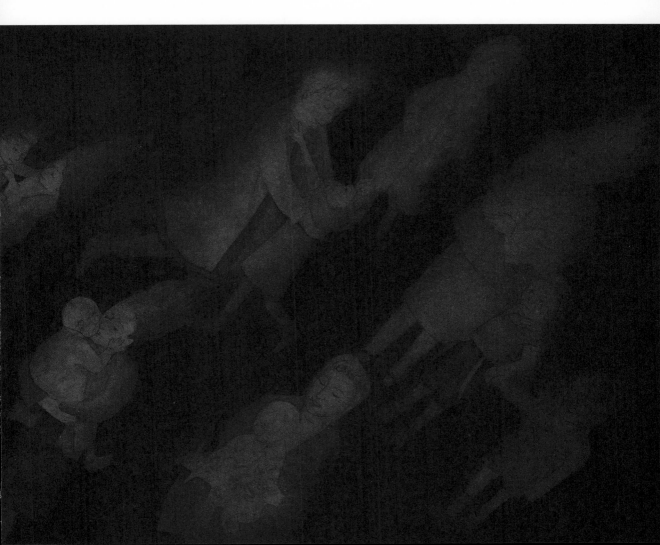

the open, as long as we cover our faces. Buckets of seawater are pulled up for us to wash with, but it makes my skin so dry, it begins to crack. One of the cooks renders cooking fat with herbs to rub into our chapped skin.

This is no cruise. Rations are meager, but we know how to survive on less than nothing. Bread and water and sleep are enough.

And love.

Almost a week in, I can feel a difference aboard. The air is decidedly balmier, but that's not all; there's a kind of buzzing energy. The captain shares the news that we are at last turning toward Haifa, just about thirty kilometers southeast. The excitement spreads and the air explodes with Hebrew and Yiddish folk songs. I understand a little Hebrew now; at the very least, I know all the words to "HaTikvah."

One of the Haganah operatives managed to get several crates of oranges at the French port. Now is the time to pass them around. The sweetness of the fruit, the sunlight, the singing are intense and heady, and the exhilaration sweeps us in. Lev pulls me up and grabs me around the waist, and we dance and sing with full force into each other's faces, hilarity in our wild eyes.

Early that afternoon, Roza tells me a rumor about a faint ship on the horizon behind us. It's been holding a straight course with the *Oasis* for hours. If it's anything other than a British ship, we're all right. The British have such a tight hold on immigration to Palestine that most of the ships that set out are turned around and their passengers sent to Cyprus, to dirty holding areas just like the concentration camps, girdled with barbed wire.

Michah finds us and confirms the rumor. "It's not completely unusual," he assures us. "Istanbul's a busy port. But let's go over the evacuation protocol again, just in case."

Hours later, Roza and I are sitting against the wall of the main cabin, sun-tired and bored, quizzing each other on math theorems. Lev's asleep beside me, his head resting on the viola case with his hat over his eyes.

Just then, whistles start blowing, and our handlers rally everyone to attention. The mystery ship is coming alongside the *Oasis*, too close to be denied any longer. It's a gray naval vessel flying the Union Jack. We know what this means. We're about to be boarded.

Guns are drawn from inside jackets and held at the ready.

"We can try again in a few weeks," Michah shouts, in an absurd attempt to reassure us. "Refugee ships get turned back all the time."

In the center of the chaos, I freeze as a string of memories scrolls across my mind—

The hasty burial of my mother. The burning city of Köln.

The screen of darkness crossing my face as the cattle-car door slides shut.

Being laid on the ground next to Lev for the first time.

The desires I've asked for over the Sabbath candles.

"Not us!" I yell. "We're going to get to Haifa if we have to jump out and swim."

"You're about to get your wish, then," Michah says.

The engines rev and we begin moving faster. We're so close to the shores of Palestine, we can practically feel the sand under our feet. When we're several hundred meters from shore, a sharp announcement crackles over the loudspeaker:

"Everyone! Gather your belongings! Leave what you don't need! Abandon ship! To the lifeboats!" Whistles and air horns sound around us as the Haganah members shepherd us, women and children, into the lifeboats. "If you are a good swimmer, and only if you *know* you can go the distance, give your things to someone you trust and go now! Now!"

The swimmers climb down the ladders. Lev takes off everything but his tzitzit and pants and gives me his clothes. I grab on to him in sudden panic.

"Lev, no! Get in the lifeboat with me!"

Roza holds me back. "You know they won't let him," she says. "He knows what he's doing."

"I'll find you, Gerta," he shouts. "You know the instructions. We'll meet on the shore. This is almost over. *Baruch Hashem!*"

With that, Lev climbs down and jumps into the open ocean.

CHAPTER 44

Yitgadal v'yitkadash sh'mei raba

—a man chants by the edge of the sea, the saltwater lapping his
ankles and pulling away into spiraling eddies—

b'alma di-v'ra chirutei,

v'yamlich malchutei b'chayeichon

uv'yomeichon uv'chayei d'chol beit yisrael,

ba'agala uvizman kariv, v'imru: Amen.

Glorified and sanctified be God's great name

throughout the world which He has created according to His
will.

May He establish His kingdom in your lifetime and during
your days,

and within the life of the entire House of Israel,

speedily and soon; and say, Amen.

Lev hasn't arrived onshore. Neither have about thirty who thought they were good swimmers. It's been two hours since we abandoned ship. The beach, miraculously, was empty, a small, cup-shaped bay where no ship could have anchored—no docks, no port. Just sand. Haganah handlers took everyone they could into hiding, including Roza, but I didn't go with them. I have to wait for Lev. Because he's coming.

I know it.

I duck inside an abandoned utility building about a hundred meters from the water. Through the small window, I watch the ocean roll, the rickety *Oasis* breaking up as it smashes against the rocks. Large, dark bubbles form on the surface of the water—the floating bodies of those who couldn't "go the distance."

Where is Lev. Where is Lev. Where is Lev. One, two, three, four, five, six, seven, eight . . .

I wait for hours in the mildewy shed, the tidewater just barely seeping in under the door. I silently practice my Wohlfahrt études, without the bow, just the fingering, simply to calm my pounding heart. Exhaustion finally overtakes me.

I wake up in a panic.

What if Lev is looking for me? Opening the door a crack, I look for anyone who might be watching to catch refugees. Not a soul is there. Only swollen bodies making

their way to the shore, carried on the drifting surf. I don't let myself look for Lev among them.

Of course he is alive. Of course he is.

He'll need the papers. He's probably there already, and he's going to need the papers.

In an instant I decide to make my way to the kibbutz. There wasn't time to write back and forth for legal sponsorship from Ruth. We can take care of that when we get there. Rifling through our bag, I find our forged papers. According to them, we're Palestinian Jews, born and married in Jerusalem, living on a kibbutz near Nahariya. Tucked into the envelope is a small piece of paper with the name of my mystery aunt and coded instructions for getting to the commune.

I start frantically shuffling down the dusty Middle Eastern road flanked by scrubby bushes. The cool morning light has given way to a blazing sun. I can't figure out, according to the instructions, how much farther to the kibbutz. I haven't had water since the ship, and the ground seems to shift and roll beneath my feet.

Just then I hear footsteps running at full speed toward me. I have nowhere to hide. I clutch the satchel and viola to my chest and brace myself for the inevitable tackle of a British soldier, the demand for papers. The footsteps stop beside me.

It is Lev.

Encrusted in dried saltwater and sand, he's panting and beginning to swoon. In the distance ahead, we see the gate to the kibbutz.

CHAPTER 45

I awake in a soft bed with clean sheets. It's hot and dry, and I'm not sweating but desperately thirsty. I've been unconscious since Lev and I collapsed together on the threshold of the kibbutz. I'm in a hut of some kind, with a glassless, shuttered window on each wall. There is a small kitchen across the room. At the foot of my bed is the bedspread that Hélène crocheted for our wedding. Lev stands at a window, his prayer shawl over his shoulders, whispering prayers he thinks I can't hear.

We must have made it. This must be our house in the kibbutz. It's tiny and spare, but it's ours. The view from the window is like nothing I've ever seen. The light is glorious and . . . full. I don't know what I expected when Michah first described it to me, but it's both exactly like I pictured and nothing like it. It's a land of blue and pale gold that goes on, blending into soft lines at the sea—not like the green fields and forests of Germany, but not like the gray, desolate camps, either.

Lev finishes his morning prayers and folds the shawl as if handling a newborn baby. I try not to distract him as I sit up in bed, but he sees me and smiles. I start to speak, but he puts his finger to his lips. He fills a pitcher of water at the kitchen sink, picks up a basin and a towel and brings them to me. He sits on the bed and looks into my face. He runs his fingers through my hair, clearing stray strands away from my neck as he recites my prayer for me.

> I thank You, O living and eternal King,
> because You have graciously restored my soul to me;
> great is Your faithfulness.

He puts the basin under my hands and pours water over them, back and forth. I cup my hands and he pours water in them, and I splash my face. He holds the pitcher to my lips, and I rinse my mouth into the basin. He dries my face and hands, and kisses my eyes, the tip of my nose, my lips and each fingertip.

This is how my first day begins in Eretz Yisrael.

CHAPTER 46

I wave goodbye to Lev as he backs the jeep out of the driveway. The wheels kick up a bit of dust, and I can't tell whether it's the aridness or his hastiness to get to Tel Aviv. Six months have gone by in an instant. It's late winter here near Nahariya, but the rains have been sparse.

Lev has started a newspaper on the kibbutz. He'll be away for three days buying parts for a salvaged printing press. I'll miss him, but I'll get to spread out in the bed by myself, a relief in this heat.

This is an old kibbutz, and there are some members who've been here from its beginning. They don't all like us. Some think we've brought too much "baggage," and they don't want to hear our stories. They wish we'd move on and be quicker about our work.

My aunt Ruth knows better, though. She helps us talk about the predicament we're in: robbed of family, marrying strangers, bringing babies into a world that tears them from their mothers' arms.

This morning, the group of us survivors gathers at Ruth's house for our monthly meeting. In the doorway, she wraps me in her tan, muscular arms and holds me in the way only an aunt can, planting a kiss on my cheek that's both soft and firm. Everyone else gets a wave or a pat on the back.

"My Gerta," she says, with her arm still around me. "Come help me in the kitchen."

Ruth and Roza and I make lemonade and put out trays of cookies while she tells funny stories about her and my father as children. She puts on records of slow jazz so we can relax before the intensity of our meeting.

"Life is good," says a Dutch woman, "freedom is good, but starvation leaves its mark, like rough rope on your wrists, always rubbing, always making a nuisance of itself."

"When I want to leave the past in the past, it follows me like a begging dog," says a man who survived five camps.

There's a shaft of morning light from the window, and I collapse into Ruth's old cracked and chafed leather chair, which is prematurely aged the same as we all were in the camps. It heaves under me as I lean over for more lemonade and another cookie. I was starved beyond recognition when the first British soldier walked through the barracks door, only thirty kilos. Now I eat, and eat.

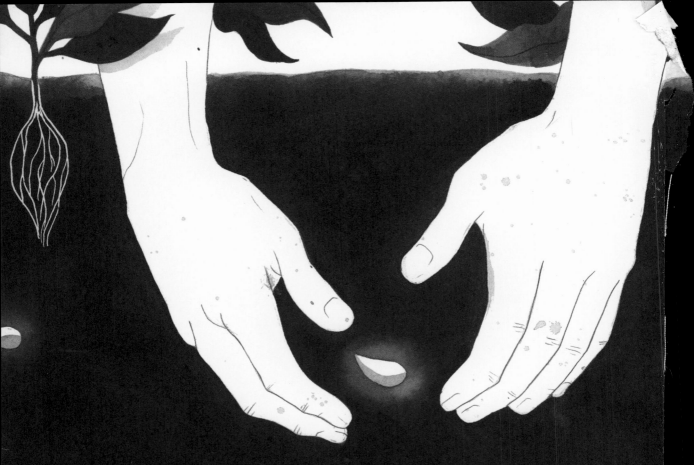

Fullness has only emptiness to compare itself to.

I eat for more than myself—I eat for six million. It's soul food, eternal nourishment—served, as it is, alongside bitterness. But I love to fill my mouth with the sweetness of freedom.

What can a girl do who has refused to die?

The meeting ends and morning work begins. We are planting a new orange grove.

The heat is subsiding a little, but I'm more woozy planting today than on even the hottest days. Still, we get through by singing. Twenty members of the kibbutz are on our team. We each strap two canteens of water on our belts and dig. We'll dig every one of the five hundred holes by hand over the next week.

In the greenhouse are saplings a meter high, which get loaded onto the truck and driven through the dust. This is not the lush farmland or forest of Europe, but desert and wilderness, with hot, salty ocean wind that sucks the moisture from our lips. I lower a baby orange tree into a hole, and my partner shovels the dirt back over the root ball.

It's too hot to continue past noon. We all go back to our homes to wash

and rest. But I grab a pad of manuscript paper and head back out. I'm ener-
gized by a new project: I am collecting songs.

The Jews here are from all over the world: Ashkenazim from Europe;
Sephardim from Spain, Africa, Greece; Mizrahim from the countries here
around us; Americans; Sabras, who've been here for millennia—all with their
own languages. We sing Hebrew songs at our meetings, but usually someone
will share one from their childhood, in their native tongue.

And a change is happening. I'm playing viola less—it's been under the
bed for days now—and I'm singing more. All the time, in fact, in the meetings, special concerts, gatherings with other kibbutzim. And the songs filling
my mind and mouth are these Jewish songs.

Last week, I told the cultural chairwoman about my idea of compiling a
songbook, and she agreed to let me and Roza do it. Lev's going to typeset it
on a cream paper, with an orange cover. We'll call it *HaEtz Tapuz—The Orange
Tree*.

Roza and I go from door to door, about five households a day, to notate
the songs. Aunt Ruth speaks several languages and comes with us to trans-
late. Not everyone is a good singer, to put it kindly, but it's fun, and I go home
each day feeling more connected to my new family. My thirsty roots feel
planted in the ground for the first time.

CHAPTER 47

I'm sitting at Ruth's table, and the sun is hanging low over the sea. The Sabbath is coming, but I've been too busy to prepare. To be honest, when it's just me alone in the hut, I get lazy about it. I wish I had Lev's fervor.

Ruth and her husband aren't religious. They don't work on the Sabbath, but they have a fairly loose understanding of what constitutes "work" anyway and usually spend their free time dancing to jazz records.

"Gerta," she says as we dip bread into a dish of olive oil, "I have something for you." She hands me an envelope and takes down her long braid. Her thick silver hair falls over her dark shoulders, and she gathers and plaits it again.

"I never get mail, except Maria's letters," I say. "What is it?"

"Open it and see," she says, with an enigmatic smile.

" 'Dear Ms. Rausch,' " I read aloud. " 'It is with pleasure that I extend you an invitation to audition for the fall semester at Tel Aviv Conservatory. . . .'

"Aunt Ruth! What is this?"

She pours me another glass of lemonade. "Well, we can't let a flower wilt away in the desert sun, can we?"

"But what about Lev?" I immediately think of the impossibility. "I can't just leave—"

"He knows. He's not just picking up equipment in Tel Aviv. Things are in motion." She winks.

I don't jump up and down about this. No, all the possibilities seep into me slowly. I cover my mouth and stare at the satisfied face of my father's sister. Quietly I get up and nestle myself next to her in her chair and wrap my arms around her entirely.

O<small>UT OF FOREST FIRES COME NEW AND STRONGER SAPLINGS</small>, reads a tapestry above the kitchen sink, embroidered with orange blossoms and fruit.

A mother outside shouts to her children that it's time to come inside and wash up, and I realize that I have to get back to light the Sabbath candles. I embrace Ruth again, gulp down my lemonade and run home, yelling a hasty goodbye over my shoulder.

I scrub my face and hands from the heat and dust and pull on my special Sabbath blouse, a dark gray gauzy one with black flowers. As I fasten the iridescent black buttons, I catch notice of the number tattooed on my arm—*A28865*—from the day I lost my name in a distant world. I draw my breath in deeply and drink in the cooling air. A sweet taste is in my mouth like honey.

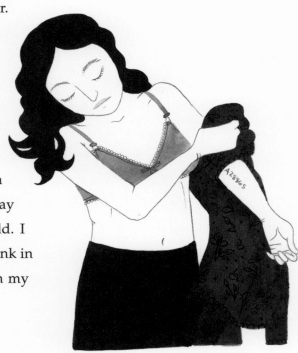

Quickly, though, my smile fades as I look out the open door. The first star has appeared in the sky.

The matches are lying next to the silver candlesticks on the table. The challah loaves are still in their box from the bakehouse, the wine bottle sealed. I've missed the start of the Sabbath.

What would Lev say? I've never asked him—can I light the candles after sunset? What would he do?

I stand in front of the unlit candles. There's still a lot I don't know about Lev—or about how to do this "grown-up" business. Some things we remember from our fathers, but no one taught us what it meant to run a home, to build a new life. No one told me what to do if I missed lighting the Sabbath candles before sunset.

What do I do now?

I watch the second star appear in the deepening blue black outside. My pulse rushes through my neck to my chest like a song. And before I know exactly what I am doing, I'm striking the match.

I wave the flames' light in toward me slowly. With my eyes covered, I feel it again: this mysterious presence, like a stranger you keep spotting in unconnected times and places. A delicious breeze blows in from the open door and ruffles the lace covering my head. *Ask for the desire of your heart.* I lower my hands and open my eyes, and the flames dance before me. I am transfixed by the light.

Suddenly something pulls me toward the twilight. I turn and run out the door, past the grove, the tractor, the community building, past the houses and the reservoir ditches and out onto the cliff overlooking the sea. The moon is huge on the horizon, just shy of full, and it shines a silver road on the surface

of the water. The sensation I'm feeling bursts forth from my lips. I'm laughing, so hard that I fall onto the ground in a wild delirium, and my cheeks hurt with a delightful pain. Rolling and groaning with exhausted joy, I grow still, lying on my side, watching the moon rise, and I fall asleep here, alone on the edge of the world.

A SONG OF ASCENTS

When the Lord restored the fortunes of Zion, we were like
    those who dream.
Then our mouth was filled with laughter, and our tongue with
    shouts of joy; then they said among the nations, "The Lord
    has done great things for them."
The Lord has done great things for us; we are glad.
Restore our fortunes, O Lord, like streams in the Negev!
Those who sow in tears shall reap with shouts of joy!
He who goes out weeping, bearing the seed for sowing, shall
    come home with shouts of joy, bringing his sheaves with him.

Psalm 126

AUTHOR'S NOTE

The summer before I entered eighth grade, I emerged from sleepaway camp with a new understanding of myself. It was as though someone opened the door and said, "You don't need to apologize for yourself anymore. Walk out into the sunshine." This newfound self-acceptance came from a single source: *music*. My camp counselor had Tracy Chapman and Edie Brickell on repeat, and it was like hearing an echo of my own voice. I eventually went to an arts high school in Manhattan with other young artists and musicians, building for ourselves deep identities based on ability and aspiration.

There's a problem with that, however. When you decide early on who you "truly are," it can trick you into thinking that you were destined to live by a certain script. And when you're out on your own and you realize that there *is* no script, you might panic.

Several years ago, I was rear-ended by a texting driver, which resulted in my arm being partially paralyzed. I completely lost the ability to play guitar—I had been a touring musician—and it took me a full year of rehab before I could reliably draw again. I had to relearn everything, even how to lift a fork to my mouth. *This wasn't in the script.* A huge element of my deeply ingrained identity had been smashed. Like Gerta, I had hinged my future on a set of expectations, which depended on life's machine running with no glitches. Being disabled cast a pall over every area of my life: my ability to drive, hold a baby, cook, hug or shake hands, let alone create art and music. How could I live my life? Without my script, who *was* I?

When my neurosurgeon gave me the unfortunate news that my paralysis was permanent, I did something that, given the extent of my injury, didn't quite make sense: I applied to graduate school for a master's in illustration. Whether it was to find another way to draw that wouldn't hurt so much or something else, I wasn't sure, but it felt like *moving forward,* and that's the only thing I knew to do.

In the first semester of our master's program, we were given the assignment of illustrating a book. I had previously written albums' worth of songs and poetry—I had even written a novel, which sat in a drawer somewhere—but I had never thought of myself as a "writer." I thought I'd illustrate a classic, like *Jane Eyre* or the *Arabian Nights,* or that I'd write a few lines about something that interested me, and lean more heavily on pictures to tell the story.

One night, my family and I were watching *Fiddler on the Roof,* one of my favorite musicals, and it occurred to me that even though I had grown up in a Jewish home in New York City, my family never discussed the persecution of the Jewish people: not the pogroms, not the Holocaust, not Israel, not the reason my stepfather's relatives came to the U.S. So I did what one does—I looked it up on the Internet.

Surprisingly, I found very little on the Russian pogroms that inspired Sholem Aleichem to write the stories upon which *Fiddler* was based, but I did find a documentary on the three-year period between the end of the Holocaust and the founding of the modern state of Israel. I had never connected the two, and I was fascinated by the human stories behind this seldom-discussed era. The fact that survivors, after losing everyone they loved, made the seemingly illogical decision to get married and bring new children into the world—this seemed to me the absolute bravest act I had ever heard of. At the core of what it means to be human is the ability to choose not just to survive, not just to hope, but to love. A fire rose up in me to tell this story.

It started as a short story for my book project, accompanied by some blocky linoleum prints, just to experiment. But the printmaking process proved too stressful on my injured arm, so I tried ink wash, which has no physical resistance. I really connected to it; with this technique, I could better convey the delicacy of a love story, and it had a kind of newspapery feel to it. I started to take advantage of this to propel the story. We have all seen the newsreels and photographs of the horrors of the Shoah. Using a similar archival look, but with metaphorical, poetic imagery, allowed me to appeal to the heart—not just the mind—of the viewer.

"Under Roots." First version in linoleum print (left); final version in ink (right).

My filmmaker husband and I were watching a lot of "slow cinema" at the time, directors like Tarkovsky and Tarr and Bergman, who reduced the speed of their shots and allowed them to rest in careful compositions that were like paintings. These black-and-white films, with their high contrast, were a huge inspiration to me. I had always worked in very bright colors, but working in black and white helped me to focus on the most important elements of the paintings—emotion, light, and silhouette—without getting caught up in color decisions. It completely changed the way I approached my work, and was a lot less strenuous on my injury, to boot. At this point, the writing had quickly evolved from an experimental short story to a full-fledged novel and was now my obsession. I was grateful to be in New York, where I had access to great libraries and museums. I could hold the archived papers of survivors, read their stories firsthand, and even spend time with some who had lived it.

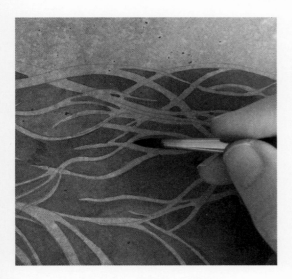

Laying down many layers of ink for the roots in "Planting Hands."

It became apparent that I needed to visit the places I had written about, and on my spring break, my friend Noelle and I rented a car and drove through three countries in five days. We started in Germany, where I was born, and traced Gerta's journey: Würzburg, Bergen-Belsen, Terezín (Theresienstadt), and Auschwitz. I don't have a lot of words to describe the experience. My friend and I simply tried to walk alongside my characters as much as we could. It felt like our arms were full of souls, and all we could do was hold them, and remember.

In Auschwitz, by one of the ruined crematoria, we came upon a Jewish youth group from England who were conducting a memorial service. In a wheelchair was a survivor whose entire family had been murdered in the very building in front of us. The rabbi invited anyone with relatives who had been killed in the Shoah to come up and give their relatives' names. Most of the teenagers there rose to give a name, or several. These were recited loudly, with reverence. As I sang with them, I felt that whatever twists and turns my own journey had taken, it had been entrusted to me to bear witness in the way that *I* was equipped to do. I couldn't do much, but I could write; I could draw. And I could invite others to remember with me.

Train tracks and crematorium in Terezín (left). The poplars reminded me
of the trees I had been painting (right).

The talents I'd put so much stock in when I was younger didn't have the same weight anymore, not for me personally; they became tools. My identity ceased to have much to do with abilities or labels. As Gerta's character revealed herself, I became conscious of the ways in which each of us, myself included, is faced with an ever-unfolding series of quandaries about our identity—the theft of it; the shedding of it; the adoption of temporary ones; the resurrection of ourselves in new forms. When we emerge from the realization that there never was a script, does it upend us completely, or present new opportunities for growth? Can we become larger than ourselves? As Hélène suggests to Gerta, there is an essence of who we are that runs deeper than what we do or what we imagine ourselves to be.

Walking the direct path from train platform to crematorium in Auschwitz, taken by countless mothers and children.

When all is stripped away, who am I? When this question comes to you, which it did for survivors like Gerta, which it will for each one of us, it shows the foundation upon which you've chosen to build, your concept of who you are in the world. Even if our abilities are diminished or removed from us, there are deeper gifts we can give. We can love others with our very selves.

GLOSSARY

PRONUNCIATIONS

Gerta Rausch (GARE-tuh roush)

Lev Goldszmit (lev GOLD-shmit)

Maria Büchner (ma-REE-uh BOOSH-nur)

Klemens Rausch (KLEH-munz roush)

Rivkah Gottlieb (RIV-kuh GOT-leeb)

Michah Gottlieb (MEE-khah GOT-leeb)

Hélène (ay-LEHN)

Würzburg (VEERTZ-burg)

Köln (koaln)

Kielce (KYELL-tzuh)

Nahariya (na-ha-REE-uh)

TERMS USED IN THIS BOOK

À bientôt (French): "See you later."

Ahnenpass (German): "Ancestor passport." An official document in Nazi Germany showing Aryan lineage.

Arbeit macht frei (German): "Work makes you free." An example of Nazi manipulation of language. This slogan hung over the entrances to several concentration camps in order to deceive prisoners into thinking that they were

entering labor, rather than death, camps, or that they could earn back their
freedom through work.

Aufwachen (German): "Wake up."

Baruch Hashem (Hebrew): "Bless the name [of God]."

concentration camp: A facility, most notably during World War II, in which large
    numbers of prisoners are "concentrated" into a small area in order to be
    controlled. There were approximately 40,000 concentration camps in the
    territories occupied by Germany during the war. Some were "death camps,"
    which were specifically used to exterminate prisoners. Most were forced labor
    or transit camps. Auschwitz was a three-camp complex with forced labor and
    extermination components, while Bergen-Belsen was originally intended as
    a holding or transit camp; however, when the Nazis evacuated other camps
    at the end of the war, they often used Bergen-Belsen as a destination for their
    prisoners.

displaced persons camp: Known today as a refugee camp, it's a place for those
    displaced by war to await resettlement. Bergen-Belsen concentration camp
    was transitioned into a displaced persons camp (using the SS military barracks
    nearby), and was the largest DP camp in Germany after the war. It remained
    open until 1950.

dramatischer Koloratursopran (German): "Dramatic coloratura soprano." A term
    describing vocal range and quality in the German *Fach* system of operatic
    classification. Singers in this category have rich, full-bodied voices with great
    acrobatic ability.

Eretz Yisrael (Hebrew): "Land of Israel." A term used to describe the biblical territory
    of Israel.

Goldszmit: Henryk Goldszmit was the actual name of Polish-Jewish pediatrician
    Janusz Korczak, who refused to leave the almost two hundred orphans in his
    care, and went with them to their deaths in Treblinka.

Haganah (Hebrew): "The Defense." A paramilitary group in pre-state Israel. Part of
    their activities included smuggling refugees out of Europe to Palestine in a time
    of severely restrictive British policies.

"HaTikvah" (Hebrew): "The Hope." Now the Israeli national anthem, its lyrics are
    adapted from a poem from the late 1800s that speaks of the hope of return to Israel.

Kaddish (Aramaic): "Holy." A hymn of praise to God, used in Jewish liturgy. Specifically, the Mourner's Kaddish, said for the deceased. The prayer makes no mention of death; rather, it extols God's attributes, signifying that even in death, God is still deserving of praise.

Kapo (German): A fellow concentration camp prisoner, often chosen from the criminal element, given privileges in exchange for policing the other prisoners under his or her charge.

kibbutz (Hebrew): "Gathering." A collective community, usually agricultural, in Israel.

Liebchen/Liebling (German): A term of endearment meaning "little love."

maestra (Italian): The female form of "maestro"—"master." "Maestro" would be used to address a conductor or musician of great renown.

Mazel tov (Hebrew): "Good luck."

mein Herzchen (German): A term of endearment meaning "my little heart."

mikvah (Hebrew): A Jewish ritual bath.

Palestine: The name of the region that today comprises the State of Israel and the Palestinian territories.

Sabbath: The seventh day of the week, on which observant Jews cease work for a day of rest and spiritual reflection.

Schnell (German): "Hurry."

Schwein (German): "Pig." Often used as a slur.

Shoah (Hebrew): "Destruction." Another term for the Holocaust.

tallit (Hebrew): "Prayer shawl." The *tallit katan* is a simple garment worn by men under the shirt. **Tzitzit** are attached to the four corners of the garment and typically worn outwardly. The *tallit gadol* is the large prayer shawl placed over the head and shoulders during prayer.

tichel (Yiddish): A scarf worn as a head covering by observant Jewish women as a sign of modesty.

tzitzit (Hebrew): Long, knotted tassels attached to a prayer shawl or a garment worn by observant Jewish men.

Żyd, brudny, nieczysty (Polish): "Jew, dirty, nasty."

EUROPE AND THE BRITISH MANDATE OF PALESTINE

1935–1947

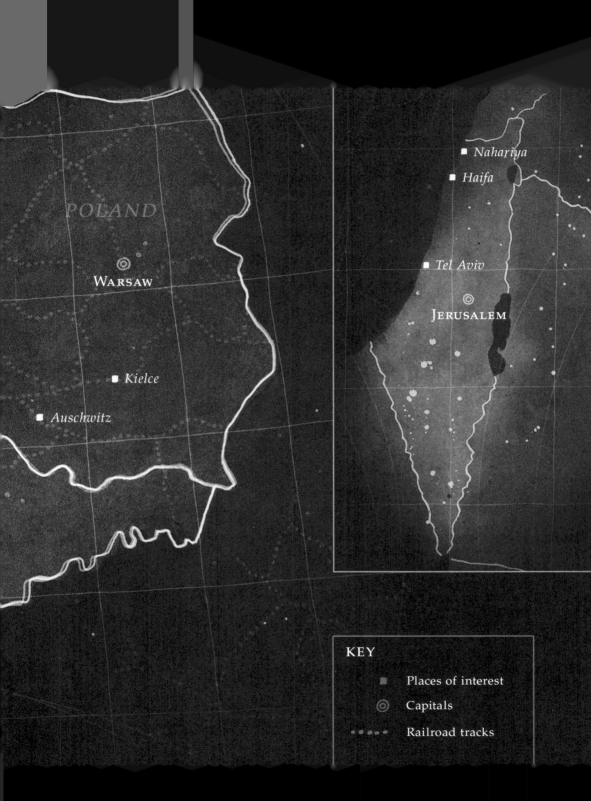

POLAND

◎ WARSAW

■ *Kielce*

■ *Auschwitz*

■ *Nahariya*

■ *Haifa*

■ *Tel Aviv*

◎ JERUSALEM

KEY

■ Places of interest

◎ Capitals

••••• Railroad tracks

RESOURCES

FILMS

The Boy in the Striped Pajamas (2008)
The Long Way Home (1997)
Schindler's List (1993)

BOOKS

This is a suggested list of books readers can use to further their understanding of the Holocaust.

Frankl, Victor E., *Man's Search for Meaning*

Konner, Melvin, *Unsettled: An Anthropology of the Jews*

Lasker-Wallfisch, Anita, *Inherit the Truth, 1939–1945: The Documented Experiences of a Survivor of Auschwitz and Belsen* (Lasker was a member of the Women's Orchestra of Auschwitz.)

Volavková, Hana, Ed., *I Never Saw Another Butterfly: Children's Drawings and Poems from Terezin Concentration Camp, 1942–1944*

Wiesel, Elie, *Night*

WEBSITES

chabad.org: (A wealth of information about Jewish beliefs and practices)
ushmm.org: United States Holocaust Memorial Museum
yadvashem.org: Yad Vashem, The World Holocaust Remembrance Center

PLACES TO VISIT

Auschwitz-Birkenau, Oświęcim, Poland

Bergen-Belsen Memorial, Lohheide, Germany

Theresienstadt, Terezín, Czech Republic

United States Holocaust Memorial Museum, Washington, D.C.

Würzburg Residence Palace and Gardens, Würzburg, Germany

Yad Vashem, Jerusalem, Israel

MUSIC

This is a catalog of the music mentioned in this book, cited alphabetically by composer.

Bach, Johann Sebastian: "Erbarme dich" and "Kommt, ihr Töchter" from the *St. Matthew Passion*

Bach, Johann Sebastian: *Wachet auf*

Bizet, Georges: *Carmen*

Carissimi, Giacomo: "Vittoria, mio core!"

Imber, Naftali Herz, and Samuel Cohen: "HaTikvah"

Mahler, Gustav: "Ich bin der Welt abhanden gekommen" from *Rückert-Lieder*. (I especially recommend Jessye Norman's moving performance.)

Mizzy, Vic, and Manny Curtis: "My Dreams Are Getting Better All the Time"

Puccini, Giacomo: *Turandot*

Schumann, Robert: "No. 1, Der Schmied: Ich hör' meinen Schatz" from *Im Schatten des Waldes*

Schumann, Robert: "Träumerei," "Hasche-Mann," and "Von fremden Ländern und Menschen" from *Kinderszenen*

Warshawsky, M. M.: "Oyfn Pripetchik"

ACKNOWLEDGMENTS

Any diligent student of the Holocaust leaves something of herself wandering in the wilderness, the soul rubbed raw in a way that may never heal, nor would she want it to for the sake of bearing witness. One cannot confront the world's greatest evil and not be changed at one's very foundation.

The two-and-a-half-year process of creating this book left me a different person. The work of being an artist and writer is, by nature, solitary, and isolation is a real occupational hazard, especially when dealing with dark subjects like this. After signing the contract for this book, I entered a period of profound loneliness that alerted me to the need for close relationships in advance of bringing the book into the public eye. I realized the importance of intentionally cultivating a close support network who know and accept me as I am, and who understand the nature of the work I do.

Chief among these are my husband, Ben Stamper, and my two children. They not only endured the two years of my grueling graduate school schedule, they did it with heaps of grace and encouragement. They were balm to my soul at the end of long days, and a reminder of love and hope.

My mother and stepfather, Eileen and Richard Braun, gave me the gifts of a Jewish upbringing, intellectual rigor, and early independence. My grandfather Ronald Young and grandmother Marge Young took me seriously when I said I would be an artist, and plunged headlong into that life with me. God placed me in just the right family, and I'm grateful.

This book began as a graduate project at the MFA Illustration as Visual Essay program at the School of Visual Arts in New York City. The assignment was to create an illustrated book on any topic of interest, and what began as a short story illustrated with twelve linoleum prints became this novel. My faculty, especially professors Marshall Arisman and Michele Zackheim, held my feet to the fire and patiently guided me as I was transformed in my approach to visual narrative. They challenged me never to settle for the expected, and to fully trust my voice.

My agent, Lori Kilkelly at Rodeen Literary Management, is a champion of my work and a woman of true generosity, a friend as well as a colleague. Every author-illustrator should be so lucky to have an agent like her.

My editor, Karen Greenberg, and art directors Stephanie Moss and Alison Impey, trusted me with creative freedom as we shaped the book together. Karen has a true gift of encouragement, in addition to her gifts in shaping stories. With Melanie Nolan, Jenny Brown, and Martha Rago, and my copy editors—Artie Bennett, Janet Frick, Amy Schroeder, and Judy Kiviat—I am blessed with an amazing team at Knopf.

Noelle Rhodes accompanied me, as few friends would, on a three-country road trip across Europe as we set foot on the sacred soil where millions perished. She served not just me, but this book. Both Noelle and Mary Hampson Patterson, PhD, lived it with me as we talked through the lives of the characters, who were as real to them as to me. Mary lovingly helped me with the deeper nuances of the book with her expert knowledge of the Holocaust, its causes and effects, and her rich understanding of human nature. Noelle and Mary's love for me is woven through these pages. It is their book, too.

Renate Evers at the Leo Baeck Institute, Center for Jewish History, led me in my research and was a compassionate help to me as I started the project. Dr. R. Steven Notley guided my grasp of the history of the modern state of Israel and its unique dynamics. Katja Seybold and Klaus Tätzler at the Bergen-Belsen Memorial allowed me access to treasures and insights that could only be obtained in the place where these events happened.

Elisha Mlotek not only modeled for the character of Lev, but sat with me, listened to my personal history with Judaism, and offered deep answers to my tangle of questions about observance and the Jewish heart. It was he who proposed the question: "What do you want your Sabbath table to look like?" His band, Zusha, does gorgeous, modern expressions of *niggunim*, wordless Hasidic melodies that transcend and lift the soul heavenward. Check them out.

In addition to Elisha, Lea Fulton, John Mosloskie, and Suzanne Greene brought Gerta and Lev (and other characters) to life through their modeling. Lea and John were especially fearless as they physically embodied the characters.

Troy Bronsink provided me with spiritual direction in which I was able to allow myself to connect with Gerta's struggle, and helped me better understand the embodiment of trauma. Peggy Gormley gently steered me away from entering *too* fully into Gerta's life when it started to wear me down. As a seasoned actor, Peggy told me that it's okay to give ninety percent—because those artists who truly give one hundred percent are the ones who lose their minds. (That's good advice.)

Elena Berkovitz and Miriam Wolkenfeld Cohen survived against all odds to welcome their great-grandchildren into the world. They gave me their time, their trust, and their stories. Their lives continue to be miracles.

Lastly, I must acknowledge the generation of Holocaust survivors we are losing to old age. Your courage to share your stories, to choose life, and to pass on hope is a treasure for the world. I pray I have listened well enough to present a worthy testimony to the next generation.